WAITI∧

S J MANTLE

S J Mantle

ISBN: 9798378400171

In memory of Ada Julia Susan Smith

CHAPTER 1

Present Day:

She had always been a rule-breaker, but not destructively, it was just she was ridiculously inquisitive. A thin, deeply veined hand gripped the bedside table. For Ada Brown rising unaided from her bed, was not without its challenges, but she was determined and had become adept at rolling onto her side, and pushing up with her skinny arms, this allowed her legs to fall off the edge of the divan. Sometimes she landed in a heap on the floor, but usually, she steadied herself. Sleep was a scarce commodity, so to relieve the boredom of endless wakeful hours, she'd taken to nocturnal exploring.

The room was dark, but not pitch black. To avoid using the main light, Ada reached for the torch in the top drawer of her bedside cabinet, placed there in readiness for such night-time forays. Slowly and a little unsteadily, at first, she forced her gnarled feet into a pair of sheepskin slippers; she shuffled to the bedroom door, where her quilted navy dressing gown was hanging. Shivering slightly, she was glad of its instant comfort. She paused for a moment, took a breath, and then turned the large, round brass handle; the heavy wooden door opened outwards, just enough to let the warm light of the corridor invade. She peered out; it was all clear. A smile spread across her lined face; with a racing heart, she began her journey.

"To the library, I think." She set off, a little less stiffly now, only when she reached the top of the stairs did she come to a standstill. A slight tilt of the head confirmed it was safe to continue; at least her ears had not failed her in old age. The constant sound of 'bleeping' medical equipment on the second floor was the only noise she could detect. It was a long, sweeping stone staircase. She took hold of the handrail and descended slowly. At the bottom, she turned right, then left, into a vast hallway; its high ceiling gave a sense of space, its pale marble floor hard underfoot. She stopped, then entered an immense room, her favourite, in the elegant Georgian house. Guided by torchlight, she went to the biography section. Here she reached into her dressing gown to retrieve a small, worn, brown book; she placed it back on the shelf. Several minutes later, she'd selected another title to devour. She concluded it was most satisfying to break the library rules and borrow a book on her own terms. Then, one of her father's lengthy lectures as a child came to mind, the one where he'd informed her that rules were 'for the obedience of fools and the guidance of the wise.' To this day, she wasn't completely sure whether he was telling her she was a foolish child or a wise child, but as the years passed, she was pretty sure it was the former.

Next stop, the kitchen, also on the ground floor but at the rear of the house, it had been striking in its day, a large square room with a high ceiling and stone floor. A series of other rooms led off it, the original larders, storage rooms, dairy, wine cellar and scullery. She headed to the old scullery, head chef, Mr Aubert's room. It was his haven from the main kitchen, a place to plan menus and try out new recipes. It was also warm for a log burner heated the room. Mr Aubert was a jolly, portly, fifty-something man originally from the Loire Valley, a man of good humour and a talented chef. She found the tray easily in the torchlight. What a kind man he was, they had never conversed about her night-time visits; indeed, she wasn't even sure if he knew it was her. But he had clearly noticed someone was in the habit of helping themselves to a cup of cocoa at night. So, he had taken to leaving a tray for the visitor containing a selection of delicacies, usually home-made biscuits, and a slice of cake. She sat in an old leather armchair with her feet up on the warm log burner and sipped the sweet chocolatey liquid between bites of a crumbly biscuit. She thought about how resistant she'd been at first to the idea of coming to live at Fairview House, and how initially she'd only agreed to a trial stay, and yet, here she was five years on. It hadn't taken her long to realise this place was a lifesaver.

Footsteps approached, Ada placed her cup back on the tray and got to her feet. The steps were closer now, why, she wondered, did she feel apprehensive? After all, this was her home, she could go where she liked, and she had implied permission to be in Mr Aubert's room. Perhaps it was their urgency? She looked around in the torchlight for somewhere close by to hide, for hasty movement was out of the question at her age.

There was a crack in the broom cupboard, Ada put her eye to it, the door to the scullery opened, two shadowy figures entered, but only just inside the door. They were animated, arguing perhaps, but frustratingly, they spoke in whispers. With her heart pounding, she took a deep breath, as hard as she strained, she could not make out what was being said, other than a couple of words, "You fool," and something that sounded like "detain." Then one of the two, who Ada had the feeling was a man, walked towards the sink area and appeared to drop something into the bin. Ada waited a few minutes, until all was quiet, before emerging from her hiding place. She made straight for the sink and, placing a foot on the bin peddle, she flipped the lid open. She shone her torch into its depths, at first, there didn't seem to be anything out of the ordinary, but as she leant in closer, something caught her eye. She lifted a piece of tissue with her fingertips, lying beneath it a capped hypodermic needle and an empty vial. Now she was suspicious, why dispose of these items in a kitchen bin and not in a proper sharps bin? And what was in the vial? It was impossible to read the label in the torchlight, she would have to be patient. If her age had taught her anything, it was there's a time and a place for asking questions. In the meantime, however, she used a piece of kitchen towel to lift the syringe and then the vial into one of Mr Aubert's paper cake bags she found lying on the worktop. She slid the bag into the pocket of her dressing gown. Back in her bedroom, she could see the vial had contained Fentanyl. A quick search on her laptop revealed it to be a strong opioid painkiller, used to treat severe pain and usually administered either in tablet form, as a nasal spray or a patch, but it could be injected too, although apparently this mainly occurred in hospital settings. With her curiosity aroused, she transferred the cake bag and its contents to an empty shoebox and placed it in her wardrobe.

"Good morning lazy bones," said Linda, Ada's cheerful carer as she placed a cup of tea beside her. Linda was a large lady, Ada guessed, in her early thirties, she was unmarried but living with a fella, a builder by trade. She had a striking face, luminescent skin, and long, curly brunette hair worn in a ponytail.

"If only you knew the half of it," said Ada laughing.

"I like what you've done with your hair!" Said Linda laughing as she passed Ada a mirror. As Ada surveyed her image, she giggled at her dishevelled white hair.

"Is madam breakfasting this morning in her room or the garden room downstairs?"

"Oh, in my room today, Linda, I can't be doing with Mrs Mortimer's daily pessimistic weather forecasts! They are always so depressing." Ada winked at Linda, who did not immediately reply, a shadow of a frown crossed her face.

"I'm really sorry to say Mrs Mortimer was found deceased this morning, Ada."

Ada sat bolt upright in her bed. "What? Really? But there was nothing wrong with her? It makes little sense."

"I know, it's a shock, as you can imagine Matron and Mrs Pritchard are deep in conversation. There will be an internal enquiry and rumour has it a post-mortem."

"Well, I'm truly sorry to hear of her passing, when do they think she died?"

"The GP has estimated in the early hours of this morning, between midnight and three."

As Ada savoured her soft-boiled egg, she thought about her recent encounter in the old scullery and realised this had occurred around two. She could not help wondering if the items she'd found in the kitchen bin had something to do with Mrs Mortimer's death. She told herself not to jump to conclusions, a post-mortem would determine the cause of death and no doubt conclude natural causes. Perhaps a heart attack or a brain aneurysm? But she determined to hold on to the items just in case.

A couple of days later, Ada was in the main entrance hall with an assortment of five or six other residents and carers noisily donning wellington boots, hats, gloves, and coats. There was an air of excitement, a sense of anticipation and much banter until the manager of Fairview, Mrs Rita Pritchard, appeared hands on hips, her usual stance.

"Ada Brown, what may I ask is all this noise? What's going on?"

"Madam, we are about to venture into the grounds to meet our new chickens." Said Major George Moore grinning widely from his wheelchair.

"What chickens? I don't know anything about chickens, would someone care to explain?"

"It's a long story, Rita," said deputy manager Sharon Jones, who was leaning on the door frame to her office, an amused look on her face. Sharon was smartly dressed in a navy and white striped trouser suit. She was probably in her early forties with short dark brown hair and the most engaging smile.

Ada liked Sharon very much indeed, she had empathy and worked hard to ensure all the residents were treated with dignity and kindness. She would be the perfect manager if it were not for old sour puss Pritchard.

Rita Pritchard, Ada estimated, was in her mid-to-late fifties, stick-thin, with dyed blonde hair scraped into a tight bun. She had a sallow complexion and pinched features and spoke with a heavy Glaswegian accent.

"You knew about this Sharon?"

"I did, I assumed you did as well, Mr Hinchcliffe and head gardener, Ted Smith, are all for it. As the owner, Mr Hinchcliffe has paid for the walkways to be built and for the chicken coop and run. I'm told Chef Mr Aubert is particularly excited about the eggs." Said Sharon.

"Madam, would you care to join us?" Asked Major Moore as he twirled the ends of his impressive moustache between his fingers.

"I would not, thank you anyway, George. Ada, I'm presuming this was your idea?" Said Rita, not managing disguise her disdain.

"Well, yes, it was, what could be better? Fresh air, fresh eggs, and a willing workforce to look after them."

"Ada, Ada, I suppose I should not be in the least surprised. You are so ...."

"Energetic, enthusiastic, kind, such fun." Interrupted Major Moore as he winked at Ada.

"Well, yes, all those things and so much more," said Mrs Pritchard, rolling her eyes as she watched the group walk down the hallway towards the back door. Ada and the Major led the way.

"Please don't bring any mud or chicken muck back into the house." She shouted after them. Ada turned and waved.

The following evening Ada organised a whist drive in the south lounge, the largest of three sitting rooms. It was a well-attended and raucous affair, with several residents consuming more sherry than was perhaps good for them, as well as cocktail sausages and bite-sized pork pie pieces provided by the kitchen. At the end of the evening, several residents required helping to their rooms. The most notable of whom was Maude Berry, who insisted on belting out the same line of 'Big Spender' over and over. *"The minute you walked in the joint, I could see you were a man of distinction..."* This was directed at Major Moore, who was popular with the ladies. He chuckled his way through each rendition, with what Ada considered to be increasing enthusiasm for each painful execution of the song.

The following morning Ada was summonsed to Rita Pritchard's office.

"Ada, take a seat, will you?" Rita peered at her over the top of her glasses.

Ada did as requested but took her time. Meanwhile, Rita fiddled with a pile of papers on her desk.

"I'm looking at last night's incident reports and they make quite colourful reading."

"Ah yes, last night's whist drive was a great success, so well attended," Ada replied.

"That maybe so, but to say it wasn't without incident is an understatement."

"Come on, Rita, get to the point. What's the problem with everyone letting their hair down a bit?" asked Ada.

"Oh Ada, Ada, if it were only that I would be content, but I've had reports of drunken behaviour!"

"Hardly, I will admit one or two of the residents became a little loud but, it was all extremely good-natured."

"And what about Maude Berry singing 'Big Spender' at the top of her voice and subsequently throwing up in one of our lovely art deco indoor planters?"

"I'd definitely put that down to an overconsumption of cocktail sausages," said Ada with just a hint of a smile.

"This is not funny Ada, I have a duty of care to every one of you. I put it to you she was drunk!"

"I assure you that's most unlikely for she's teetotal, has been for forty years. I'd put money on it being down to the excitement of the occasion and an overindulgence of the nibbles myself." Ada folded her arms across her body.

"Very well, as it appears you are the residents' appointed co-ordinator of activities, I must insist you give me prior notice of all planned events and, should I feel any are unsafe or inappropriate, I will veto them. Do you understand?"

"Perfectly, Rita, perfectly."

"Good, well thank you Ada and good morning to you."

During the following three weeks, Ada organised many activities for her fellow residents, she however disguised their true nature to ensure Rita Pritchard allowed them to go ahead. Line dancing became 'movement and music for the over seventies', the cheese and wine evening, a lecture on British cheeses, the murder mystery evening, a book club session in the library. And thus, life carried on as before without interference.

Detective Sergeant Harriet Lacey wondered how many times in her career she had boxed up the contents of her desk at the end of an inquiry. Operation Juliet had been a tough case, originally viewed as a double murder, perhaps a domestic gone wrong, it soon spiralled into a complex number of killings linked by DNA. For it transpired one victim and two of the killers were triplets. One offender, Joe Wilson, remained at large. Harriet did not doubt they would catch him in the future based on her view he was a sociopath with heightened traits of self-importance. She figured he could not stay in the background. He needed to be noticed. The burning question, however, was when would he re-surface?

Harriet's mobile sprang into life, she glanced at the screen; it was Detective Chief Superintendent Derek Wynn. Harriet had worked with Derek for several years. He was calm, good-looking, and kind. A gentleman and skilled detective to boot. There had been a time early on when she'd wondered if they might have a future together, but then her life changed, and she changed.

"Afternoon, Harriet, I apologise for the short notice, but I need you for a sensitive inquiry. There's been a death at a Fairview Residential Home; it's caused quite a stir. The deceased, a Major George Moore, has died unexpectedly. Yesterday, he had a full private medical and was determined to be in rude health. It now appears there are rumours of other unexplained deaths at Fairview, as well as other incidents of concern. I don't need to tell you how delicately we are going to have to tread, and I have the gut feeling it will be a complex case. I'll explain all when I see you; shall we say three in my office?"

What Harriet wondered was what Derek Wynn was alluding to; her interest sparked.

CHAPTER 2

407 AD - The Forest of Dean Gloucestershire:

The hunter kept low, stepping lightly on the forest floor, pausing every so often to listen for movement, surveying their prey as they crept towards it. Placing one knee on the ground, they stealthily reached for an arrow, which they placed across the centre of the bow. Staring down the length of the shaft, they pulled back the bowstring, releasing the arrow into the misty morning air. Amid the Silence, a thud. The hunter ran towards their kill, a magnificent red deer.

Odell punched the air in triumph before turning and running back to the clearing where her father's horse waited patiently. Untying the old grey, she led him on. Although small in stature, she was strong, wiry, and agile. Deftly, she trussed up the deer carcass with rope made from nettle fibre, straining with the effort, she heaved it onto the sledge at the rear of the horse, and tied it to the structure next to the rest of her bounty, four rabbits and a basket of forest mushrooms.

On the journey back to the settlement, Odell picked chestnuts from the forest floor. Their savagely sharp outer husks jabbed into her fingers, causing her to curse as one drew blood. With her basket full, she continued winding in and out of the trees, a well-worn route. The path, wet and slippery, started to climb, causing the old horse to stumble. Finally, she reached the top of the hill, where her extended family awaited her return.

Defences, earthen banks, and ditches with sharpened timber stakes enclosed their land and houses. Her customary whistle brought her little brother Alwin running to the impressive entrance gate. He let her into the compound before securing the gate behind her. Odell's grandmother appeared in the doorway to their hut and waved. Within minutes, she was surrounded by other family members, who surveyed her morning's work with smiles, for they would eat well for the next few days. On entering the hut, Odell was handed a steaming bowl of barley porridge which her grandmother had topped with precious wild honey and dried hazelnuts.

"Your father would be so proud of you, without you, we would all have perished."

"I'm pretty sure that's not the case but thank you anyway, Ma."

"You know it is. "

A couple of days later, Odell was sitting beside a local forest pond about half a mile from the settlement, fishing for pike. She often sat in this spot on a mossy bank surrounded by tall pine trees, which she thought looked rather like proud soldiers standing to attention. It was a place that reminded her of happier times. When her father was taken by the Romans, she had buried her grief deep in her soul. Every so often, she allowed herself to think of the man who'd been her hero. A tall, muscular, and fearsome warrior, with a gentle side. A fair man who believed in hard work and duty to his people. How she missed his smile, his strength, his guidance. Sudden bird flight and the sound of snapping twigs alerted her to interlopers. She jumped to her feet and threw her fishing line down; she knew she must hurry, for there are many dangers in the forest. She ran up the wooded hill immediately behind her and only stopped when her legs burnt with the effort, and she could no longer draw breath. After resting for a moment, she took a deer path and doubled back on herself. After about fifteen minutes, she found herself immediately above the intruders, who were busy arguing and had failed to notice her. Odell listened to the ongoing conversation.

"You are idiots, had you only been quieter, I could have surprised Odell. Now, she's disappeared into the mist." Odell recognised the voice as that of her cousin, Alfred.

"Why do you care about Odell? Just take her as one of your women and be done with it," said a second male, known to Odell as Alfred's second in command Edgar.

"Odell does not do anything she doesn't want to." Said Alfred sighing.

"She's a woman and should know her place."

Without warning a figure leapt from a nearby tree, landing on Alfred's shoulders, glistening knife held to his throat. Alfred yelled out, the attacker was immediately surrounded by Alfred's men.

"Cousin, what brings you to these parts?" asked Odell laughing, as she nimbly jumped down from Alfred's shoulders.

Alfred was about three years older than Odell. Brought up together as children, they had known each other all their lives. He was tall and wiry, but headstrong. His ginger beard and hair were long and unkempt, he smelt of animal fat and sweat.

"There you are! Dressed as a man." Exclaimed Edgar grimacing at her.

"That's because I must do a man's job. You lot abandoned your kin, remember?"

"That's not quite true, we were boys who went in search of our men, my father, your father, their fathers, and our adult women." Alfred pointed to his men, who numbered about ten and who were noticeably avoiding eye contact with Odell. Alfred continued. "We went as soon as they were seized by the Romans to work in the forest mines. We were determined to get revenge. It's

17

just, we didn't come back, we stayed to fight for our tribe, fight the filthy Roman occupiers."

"Exactly, and thereby abandoning the wider family." Said Odell.

"It's time you aligned yourself to a man." Said, Edgar spitting on the ground.

"I have no interest in doing so. No man has caught my eye, I appear to be destined to be surrounded by weak men and strong women."

"You are your own woman certainly." Said, Alfred.

"Well, don't let me keep you, then, you've got Romans to hunt, and I have fish to catch." Odell put her knife back in its sheaf and turned to go.

"Just take her you fool." Said Edgar hands on his hips.

"He knows better than that, tell him." Odell looked directly at Alfred.

"Yes, I could take her, but she would slit my throat in my sleep." Said Alfred staring at the forest floor.

"Good, well I'm glad we understand each other." Said Odell walking off in the direction of her discarded fishing line, leaving the tribesmen open-mouthed.

Several hours later Odell had succeeded in catching three Pike but was more excited by the two wild ducks who had settled on the pond beside her, and who would not now be returning to their night-time roost. Shivering Odell pulled her cape around her, the sky had turned a thick dark menacing grey. Winter was fast approaching, bitter dark mornings, frozen water, little natural light. It meant one thing, more work, extra wood for the fires, the need to eke out their meagre stores of grain, preserved meat, and fish. Winter was a time of struggle, and not everyone in the settlement would survive.

Next morning, Odell set off with her father's horse and sledge in search of firewood. Dressed in woollen trousers held at the waist with a belt and an over-tunic. Her heavy woollen cape was fastened at the shoulder with her father's brooch. Her Grandmother had braided her dark brown hair to keep it out of her face, flat leather shoes kept her feet relatively dry.

Odell knew she must find an additional source of firewood, and that meant she would have to go further afield than usual. After about an hour of walking, the ground dipped down into a natural valley where the trees were younger, easier to cut down. As luck would have it, autumnal storms had felled several. Odell set to work, instinctively seeking the seasoned trunks to cut into lengths. Using every ounce of strength she could muster, she hauled the lengths onto the Sledge to be logged later. The less time spent in the open, the better. Although not afraid, she had learnt to be wary.

The burden of responsibility for her extended family weighed heavily on her. Aware that if something were to happen to her, the rest would perish. For they were in the main children and old women. There were no others of her age apart from Freya, who was unstable on her feet and mute. All their men and able-bodied women had been taken. Odell didn't like to dwell on their fate, for it made her forlorn. She longed for the time many seasons back when daily tasks were shared, the men hunted, and sourced wood and the women and children grew grains and vegetables and tended to the animals. And, sometimes, although not often, they would all get together to celebrate a festival. On such occasions, there would be plenty to eat, much laughter, singing and storytelling. How she longed for those times.

Brought back to the present by a peculiar noise, she listened intently, holding her breath as she did so. It seemed to have come from the far side of the wooded basin. She frowned, for it sounded like a cough. She sniffed the air and detected the faintest aroma of wood smoke. Then again, the same sound, definitely a cough. Leaving the horse tied to a tree, she drew her knife and stealthily made her way to the lip of the basin. Crawling the last bit on her stomach so that only her head appeared over the top. She gasped at what she saw, but as luck would have it, she was too far away to be heard. Beneath her, in a lightly wooded dell, were several men milling around a small campfire. She counted fifteen in all. To a man, they were in a sorry state, some stood trying to warm their blue hands with their breath, others were lying on the damp forest floor. One or two were sitting on their haunches. In the far distance, one man was active, tall, muscled, with dark brown skin, gathering firewood. Odell had never before seen such a skin colour; it was several minutes before she could tear her gaze away. A short distance from the main group and the closest to her stood a man with his back to her, head bowed in prayer or perhaps in despair? These men were not dressed for the weather conditions, thin woollen trousers over lightweight tunics and inadequate cloaks. Only their sheepskin boots offered some protection from the cold. Odell could see no cooking pot nor indeed shelter. As she stood surveying the men, white feathery flakes drifted down from the dark sky. Odell recognised she must leave, but still she remained glued to the spot. Who were these men and what were they doing in the densest part of the forest? Then the man closest to her turned and looked directly at her. They locked eyes. Odell saw he was tall, with short dark brown hair, oval green eyes, and stubble on his chin, but no beard. Not like the men of her world. There was nothing for it now but to confront him.

"Who are you?" asked a scowling Odell, hunting knife in hand.

"Are you always so direct?" asked the ashen soldier.

"You mean rude, and yes, I am." Just the hint of a smile flitted across the man's face.

"I am Centurion Maximus Augustus," said the man.

"And what are you doing in this part of the forest?"

"Waiting to die." Maximus looked at his feet.

"What do you mean? "Asked a wide-eyed Odell.

"We were stationed at the Roman fort at Corinium Dobunnorum when we were sent by the commander on a mission to this place. It was authorised by Rome. At first, all was well but, then contact with the fort suddenly ceased."

"Where is this fort you talk of?" Asked Odell.

"It is over forty miles from here." Replied Maximus.

"What was the mission you were sent on?"

"I cannot tell you, other than it was critical."

"But as you've just told me you're waiting to die, so why does it matter?"

"I'm not going to tell you."

"You're just going to give in and die?" Odell had her hands on her hips.

"Without supplies and adequate shelter, we've become ill. I sent men to Corinium to fetch help, but they did not return. This small group is all that's left of eighty men, some deserted, some died, and some did not return from Corinium. So, you see, things are hopeless."

"Not for all of you. What about that man gathering firewood?" Asked Odell, pointing.

"Marcus Atilius is a former Gladiator, Gladiators fight to the death, he refuses to give in. If it were not for him, we would already be dead."

"Well, at least one of you is showing some backbone." Said Odell shaking her head.

"You don't like the Romans?"

"Oh, worse than that, I despise the Romans."

"I'm sorry to hear that. We are not all corrupt."

"I don't believe you. Your fellow Romans took my father, all the men of my family, and all the adult women to work and die in the forest mines."

"They did?"

"Don't pretend you didn't know, you pig." Spat Odell.

"I wasn't; I was truly under the impression that work in the mines was voluntary."

"Please don't insult my intelligence." Shouted Odell. Marcus the Gladiator looked up to survey the slip of a girl giving his leader a hard time.

"I meant no insult, truly, I did not. Our commander said all workers in the mines were there of their own accord. It seems this was wrong. So, you have no men at home?"

"We do not."

"Then how do you survive?"

"Without men, you mean?" Said Odell, sneering at the soldier before her.

"Yes."

"Well enough for the past five years. The old women, girls, and boys look after the animals and grow vegetables. I hunt and gather food from the forest."

"Not by yourself? You must have help?"

Odell shook her head, a heat flushed through her. The snow was falling hard now; time to leave.

"I'm not callous, but I must leave. My family relies on me to provide for them; they are anxiously awaiting my return with firewood. I wish you well, but fear you will not last the night unless you find the will to fight."

"I do not for one minute believe you to be unfeeling. Thank you for stopping by. May I know your name before you leave us?"

"My name is Odell, after my mother and her mother."

"That's a beautiful name. What does it mean?"

"Small, wooded valley."

"How apt. May the gods protect you and your family, Odell."

She spun around and bounded up the slope, only turning as she reached the top for one last look. She locked eyes with the former gladiator.

Odell made her way back to her father's patient old horse. The snow was settling now. She would have to hurry to make it back before dark. As she set off, she thought of the men in the dell and how their lifeblood was slipping away. She hated the Romans. As she trudged along, she bit her lower lip, for the men's desperate fate played on her mind. She shivered at the truth of their situation. Tears raced down her cheeks. She'd left them to die. She should have tried to help. But practically, what could she have done? Still, the tears flowed. Life was hard, a thick-skin compulsory and the welfare of her family had to come first. She wiped her eyes on her sleeve and walked on. It was dusk now, and the forest was strangely silent, the falling snow distorted the fading light, bathing everything in a grey hue. Head down, Odell continued on; the occasional sound of a sob echoed through the trees.

CHAPTER 3

Present Day: Fairview Residential Home

Ada wept as she walked around her room in large sweeping circles, staring at the carpet. She did not want to think about George Moore, but she could not get him out of her mind. Adamant, it had not been his time to go, she felt something was amiss, but try as she might, she could not work out what. It was driving her mad. So, for the hundredth time, she went over it again in her head.

She had arrived at Major Moore's door at 0830 on the dot, as she did every Friday. She had knocked, and as every Friday, did not wait for an invitation to enter. The room was in darkness. Instead of the Major sitting in his wheelchair waiting for Ada to steer him to breakfast, he was in bed. Ada remembered making some flippant comment about missing breakfast if he didn't get a wiggle on and offering to summon his carer to help him get ready. But he did not reply, she had walked across to him, and the moment she set eyes on him, she knew he was dead. She wondered why death was so often described as a peaceful state, the deceased portrayed as serene? In her experience, it was not like that at all. She did not want to relive the vision of her friend lying rigid on his back, but she could not prevent it from permeating her thoughts. His ashen grey face, thin translucent skin stretched across his features, blue lips, a face contorted by the last throws of death. Ada shivered and shook.

"Stop it, stop it, silly woman, concentrate, try to remember." She sobbed.

There was a knock at the door. "Come in," Ada shouted as she wiped her eyes with a handkerchief hastily retrieved from a sleeve.

Rita Pritchard marched into the room with a sense of purpose, only to lose momentum and come to an abrupt halt a few feet from Ada.

"Dear Ada, I'm so sorry. I can only imagine what a shock it was finding the Major this morning, I came as soon as I got your message that you wanted to see me." Rita stepped forward and placed a hand on Ada's arm.

"Thank you, Rita, I wanted, I needed to tell you that something is very wrong, very wrong indeed. I know it is, it's just I can't put my finger quite on what it is yet, but I will. Please take the Major's death seriously. Promise you will." Ada wiped her red eyes once more.

"Ada, it's okay, please don't worry, I promise, Matron and I have alerted the police. Forensic officers are to attend, and a Home Office Pathologist will carry out a post-mortem. I always think it's better to be safe than sorry."

27

"Indeed, and thank you, Rita, I know we haven't always seen eye to eye, but I know I am right." Ada was suddenly aware of feeling light-headed, she reached out to Rita to steady herself but failed to make contact in time, dropping to the floor with some force.

Detective Chief Superintendent Derek Wynn's office:

While Derek Wynn ran through the practical details of Operation Delta, Harriet surveyed the small group of staff occupying his office. She could not wipe the grin from her face, for she had worked with these officers before and was fond of them. Her gaze settled first on seasoned detective Mike Taylor. They had not always liked each other, but they had overcome their shared antipathy and were now firm friends and colleagues, Mike was a shrewd officer. Detective Sergeant Paul Jones, or 'Jonesy' as he was affectionately known, worked in Scenes of Crime. Skilled and clever, with a large personality and a pronounced Welsh accent, he also had a perchance for brightly coloured waistcoats. He was discreet and loyal and believed wholeheartedly in teamwork. Working alongside Paul was Steven Leach, a senior Scenes of Crime Officer. Although Harriet had only worked with him once before, he had immediately impressed her with his forensic knowledge and attention to detail. A tall man, aged about thirty with great energy and a slight awkwardness but affable. And last, there was Kate Squires. Despite at least a fifteen-year age difference, they'd struck up a firm friendship. It was Kate who had saved Harriet's life after she was injured at the hands of a violent psychopath. Her ability to find digital footprints from mobile phones and laptops was extraordinary. She was now working for the Constabulary in Scenes of Crime, mentored by Paul Jones. Kate's father Henry, a successful Orthopaedic surgeon, was in Yemen working for MSF–Médecins Sans Frontières, as a result, Harriet and Kate were spending a good deal of time together. Harriet had hoped to build a future with Henry, but then he left for Yemen to carry out humanitarian work. Now things were in the balance, for it had been a new relationship and yet, each time he entered her thoughts, it sent her pulse racing, and she experienced an empty sensation in the pit of her stomach. She shifted her position in her chair and cleared her throat to get back on track.

"Fairview Residential Nursing Home on Abbey Road is a fifty-room private facility. There are a hundred and fifty full and part-time employees. The Manager, Mrs Rita Pritchard, has worked there for ten years and has kindly agreed to make herself available to officers. She has also agreed to provide an office for us to work from. This investigation will require a great deal of patience because there are many complaints/ incidents to work through. I cannot emphasise enough the importance of professionalism in this matter. You will undertake the initial enquiries so that we can establish what we are dealing with." Said Derek Wynn, fidgeting with a pile of papers.

"The first complaint is from a Mr and Mrs Graham. They attended Mill Street Police Station six weeks ago to voice their concerns that a member of staff may be responsible for assaulting Mr Graham's mother Eileen. They claim that on two separate occasions Eileen indicated to them a carer had hurt her. It was during their second visit they noticed bruising on both wrists and took photographs. They reported this to Rita Pritchard, who conducted an internal enquiry but found no evidence to support their claim of assault. Unsatisfied, they came to the police."

"What was the explanation given by Fairview for the bruising?" asked Mike Taylor, his pen poised.

"Eileen has a documented history of violence towards other residents and on occasions, in the past, she's had to be restrained. Mrs Pritchard ruled that in the absence of any other evidence this was the most likely explanation for the bruising. There are no recent reports relating to the restraint of Eileen however, and the findings which I've read, reveal that several staff members describe Eileen as frail, sometimes verbally abusive, but not physically. So, there are some obvious question marks here."

"What did Eileen say? "Asked Harriet.

"Unfortunately, Eileen has an aggressive form of dementia and is rarely lucid. I could see nothing in Rita's notes to show that she had spoken to Eileen, which is a concern, and the photographs do show deep bruising. This requires further scrutiny, something doesn't quite add up. If she is as frail as they claim then, how much danger does she pose to other residents? Enough to justify restraining her? And does she bruise easily?" Derek frowned before continuing.

"Paul, I'd like you and Steven to look at these photos and let me have your observations. Harriet, can you get hold of the policy from Fairview on restraining residents, please? "They all nodded as Derek Wynn paused to make a note in his policy document.

"Right onto the next complaint or incident, which is made by a woman called Sharon Dean. A little over two weeks ago, she rang the force control room to claim she had evidence her elderly father Stanley Cross, a resident at Fairview, was being regularly assaulted. Sharon told the operator she had placed a covert camera in Stanley's room without the permission or knowledge of the staff. Sharon has provided some limited footage which is of a poor grainy quality and unfortunately, only shows the lower half of an individual, there is no image of the person's face. It is possible, however, to make out Stanley sitting in his chair next to his bed with this person leaning over him."

"Have you studied the footage, Sir? And, if so, did it indicate foul play?" asked Harriet.

"I have looked, but not in any detail. I simply scanned it to get an idea of the allegations, it looks to me as if on several occasions Stanley is being remonstrated with, perhaps manhandled, as if a series of arguments are taking place."

"This might be a good place for me to interject." Said Mike Taylor. "I visited Stanley Cross last week as you requested, Sir. Stanley is a proud man who refused to confirm or deny ill-treatment. I got the feeling he was hiding something; I also got the feeling he was fearful of something or someone. He is judged to have mental capacity, but I think we need to tread carefully, he is vulnerable based on his age, his poor health, and my gut feeling is that there is something he isn't saying. His daughter, on the other hand, is a different kettle of fish. Fuck me, sorry, excuse my language, but she is a large lady with a large mouth and a large amount of pent-up aggression. I had the misfortune to bump into her in the reception area as she was tearing into Mrs Pritchard, who kindly passed her onto me for an update! I can't be sure, but I feel Sharon Dean may be thinking about bringing a false claim against Fairview."

"Interesting, thanks Mike, can I just say; that's the first time I've known you to apologise for swearing. There's hope for you yet, when you put your mind to it, you can be both charming and professional!" Derek Wynn and the others broke into laughter.

"Somehow, we need to move this forward, Kate and Steven; please study the footage provided by Sharon Dean. Harriet and Mike, have another chat with Stanley, would you? Perhaps somewhere other than his room, see if you can get him to feel comfortable enough to talk." Once more, Derek scribbled a note in his policy document.

"Okay, onto the next matter, the sudden death of resident Vera Mortimer. Vera died about three weeks ago. Unusually, she had no underlying medical conditions. Vera did not drink, smoke, or eat red meat. She took daily walks and took part in regular keep fit sessions. Her death came as a tremendous shock. So much so, Matron reported it to the coroner. There will be a post-mortem this week. Paul, can you please liaise with Rita Pritchard and Matron Alice Goodman and the Coroner? I'd also like you to attend the post-mortem. Whilst this death might well turn out to be natural causes, I think we need to make sure we cover all bases."

"Now to the death of Major George Moore reported to us this morning. Again, this is strange, but is it suspicious? What I will say is the Major undertook a thorough private medical yesterday, which he passed with flying colours. His death was unexpected. Steven, I'd like you to liaise with the coroner and to attend his post-mortem. Harriet, please speak to resident Ada Brown, the Majors best friend, it was she who found him this morning. Understandably, she has taken his death badly, she also thinks there is something suspicious or amiss about the Major's death. Rita Pritchard tells me Ada is usually the life and soul of Fairview, describing her as warm, effusive, energetic, and mischievous. And, hugely popular. Apparently, what she doesn't know about her fellow residents isn't worth knowing. Steven and Paul, can you please liaise with the forensic team to see if they have found anything of interest? "

"Boss, are there any further allegations or issues?" Asked Harriet.

"Yes, I received a call yesterday from the Care Quality Commission. How familiar are you all with their work?" A series of blank faces looked back. "Okay, well, they regulate and inspect health and social care services. It appears a whistle-blower who works at Fairview has contacted them."

"Bloody Hell." Said Mike.

"Indeed, now, it seems the CQC received two calls from a female with some medical knowledge. She alleged that someone at Fairview was systematically and deliberately over-medicating patients, and they were dying.

When pressed, she said she thought they had been administered with large doses of prescription painkillers, but she wasn't sure. The whistle-blower is terrified for her safety. She last called the morning after Vera Mortimer's death."

"We have quite a task ahead of us, I'd say." Said Harriet.

"I think that's the understatement of the day," teased Mike.

Ada opened her eyes to see two faces peering back at her.

"Hello Ada, welcome back." Said Linda, taking her pulse.

"What happened?" Ada pulled herself up into a seated position in her bed.

"You fainted spectacularly." Said Rita.

"Did I? Well, I'm sorry to have been a bother."

"Not at all, I think the combination of shock and a lack of breakfast or lunch may have had something to do with it."

"I agree, it's time you ate and drank something." Linda walked across the room to retrieve a tray containing dainty sandwiches, two cupcakes, and a pot of tea.

"Chef Aubert prepared this especially for you." Said Rita.

"How kind." Although still feeling strange, Ada tentatively reached for one of the bite-sized sandwiches, savouring the tarragon chicken filling. She licked her lips before helping herself to a cream cheese and smoked salmon one. Soon, Ada had eaten the entire contents of the tray. Immediately, she felt much better.

Rita left, but Linda stayed with her.

"The healing power of Earl Grey tea is truly amazing." Said Linda, laughing.

"Don't mock, young lady, it is truly wonderful!" Ada reached into her bedside table and pulled out her black- rimmed glasses, a set of notelets and a pen. Once she had scribbled a note of thanks to Mr Aubert, she handed it to Linda for delivery.

Then an overwhelming desire to close her eyes flooded over her, not something she'd experienced for a very long time. She snuggled down in the bed, by the time Linda had placed a fleece blanket over her, she was asleep.

Ada awoke at six. She could not remember the last time she had slept for so long without periods of insomnia intruding. She lay in her bed and went over the events of the day before again in her head. A feeling of loss and melancholy enveloped her, she tried to rationalise it, to fight it but, she recognised the deep-seated gloom encasing her. It was a feeling she knew all too well, a feeling she dreaded. She had just pulled the duvet over her head when Linda burst into the room.

"Good morning my lovely, now, what are you doing hiding under there?" Ada's head slowly emerged from underneath the covers.

"Right, are we having breakfast downstairs or here? Just so that you know everyone is asking after you, they send their love. They'd like to see you."

"I'm not feeling very sociable this morning."

"Breakfast in your room it is then." Linda drew back the curtain and approached the bed, Ada was aware she was being scrutinised.

"Look, I know you've lost a dear friend and you're feeling awfully sad and down, but you are not the only one. George was well-loved by all the residents. It's so quiet downstairs without you, it's full of gloomy-looking faces."

Ada shuffled up the bed and pulled herself up onto her pillow. "I'm truly sorry to hear that, but I can't summon the energy to care enough to go downstairs. I don't want to see anyone. I want to wallow in misery as selfish as that may be."

"It's not selfish Ada, it's quite understandable. You loved the Major and he loved you. Life was great until suddenly it wasn't, and now he's no longer here, leaving you wondering how to live without him."

Ada didn't respond because she could not deny it.

A week passed, and still Ada refused to leave her room or receive visitors. One morning after breakfast, Rita Pritchard arrived.

"Good morning, Ada." She boomed in her loud Glaswegian accent. "What in heaven's name are you doing sitting there in a wheelchair? Is there something wrong with your legs?" Ada shook her head but did not turn to face Rita, then the penny dropped. "Och, you're in the Major's chair." Ada nodded as she continued to stare out of the window.

"Look Ada, we are worried about you, you haven't left your room in a week, you are not eating enough to keep a sparrow alive, you are not receiving guests. Indeed, you are so out of sorts, I've asked matron to visit you." Ada jerked her head around and gave Rita a harsh stare before shrugging her shoulders.

Half an hour later, Matron duly arrived to carry out her assessment, Ada was waiting for her, and before Matron had the chance to set foot over the threshold, Ada took the initiative.

"Matron, I'll save you the trouble, I am suffering from a bout of the blues, I'm down in the dumps, miserable, broken-hearted. And that's all there is to it. It will either pass, or it won't, there's nothing to be done. Now please shut the door behind you and leave me to it, I'm busy waiting to die." Matron raised her eyebrows and took a step forward, it looked to Ada as if she was about to say something, so Ada stuck her tongue out, this did the trick; Matron turned and hastily left the room.

407 AD - The Forest of Dean Gloucestershire:

A series of high pitch screams penetrated the early morning air, so jarring, they triggered a howling frenzy from the settlement dogs. Sleepyheads appeared at hut doors.

Odell was the first to emerge, her bow primed, she looked around for the source of the danger; she spotted Freya rooted to the spot at the entrance to one of the animal huts, her hands covered her open mouth. Odell ran across and placed her arms around her.

"Oh Freya, you can speak, or at least scream, how wonderful." A mixture of sounds, emanated from Freya, as she fixed Odell with a wide-eyed gaze.

"This is all my fault, I'm sorry to frighten you, I was so late home last night, so cold and tired, I should have expected this." Odell held Freya closer.

After several minutes, Freya pulled away and pointed to the entrance of the hut, eyebrows raised. "Yes, you're right, I should explain and, I will, but could we go to the long hut to get out of the cold?" Freya nodded.

"Come on everyone to the long hut, all of us," shouted Odell. As everyone started to move off, trudging through the snow, Odell turned and beckoned. After a moment or so a figure appeared from one of the huts, followed by another and another. Ma did not move from the side-line, hands on hips.

"What in the name of the gods have you done?" she hissed.

"Ma, I had no choice, come into the warm and I will explain." But Ma remained where she was, "Filthy Romans."

Odell jerked her head at the irate show of emotion, tentatively she walked towards her grandmother and took Ma's hand in hers. Tiny, wrinkled and red raw, the result of a lifetime of hard work.

"Ma, I came across these Romans quite by chance while gathering firewood yesterday. They were a pitiful sight, emaciated, devoid of hope, just waiting to die. At first, I felt nothing but anger and hate towards them for all the hurt they have inflicted on us, but, as we talked, things changed. As I made my way back to the settlement, I could not stop weeping, I could not reconcile the feeling I was responsible for their impending deaths, so I turned around and retraced my steps. It was then I struck a deal that will benefit us all. The least you can do before you judge me is to come and hear the details of our pact."

Ma let out a loud huff but followed on behind. A sea of expectant faces greeted Odell, on one side of the hut stood her family huddled together for safety, on the other, a group of men bedraggled and gaunt. One stood head and shoulders above the rest, Marcus Atilius, the former Gladiator. Odell noticed he wore a large animal tooth on a leather string around his neck, he smiled, and she acknowledged this gesture with a nod of the head before turning to face her family.

"I know you must be confused and frightened by the sudden appearance of these men in our settlement, but I assure you will come to see this is a good thing." As Odell scanned the hut, she realised her family was far from convinced, she would have to try harder.

"Look, it's complicated, but not all of us will survive this winter. I alone cannot find sufficient food to feed us. However, with these men's help, we may make it through. All they request in return is food and shelter. In the spring, they will leave. I have made it clear that should any of them step out of line, they will suffer dreadfully. "

"How do we know we can trust them? After all, they are stinking Romans." Asked Ma. Before Odell could answer, a man got to his feet.

"I am Centurion Maximus Augustus, the leader of these men. We are indebted to you for taking us in, for saving our lives; if Odell had not led us here last night and allowed us to shelter with your animals, most of us would not have woken this morning. I promise we will not let you down, but will work to ensure we all flourish. And, when spring comes, we will leave. The Roman army has wronged you in the past, and I can only apologise, but I assure you we will give you no cause for alarm."

"Thank you, Maximus, now everyone, we have work to do. There are empty huts to clean and restore, and these men need to wash and have suitable clothes found for them; they also need feeding, then we can think about getting on with our daily chores."

As everybody departed, Odell saw out of the corner of her eye, her little brother Alwin, take Marcus by the hand. This slight gesture of kindness did not go unnoticed by the others.

As the days passed, the Romans became stronger and helped with everyday tasks. For the first time in years, there was chatter and laughter as the settlement children found their voices again. Occasionally, the Roman soldiers would play tag with them or give them piggyback rides. The men also helped to fetch water and firewood, to tend to the animals and repair sections of the settlement ramparts, holes in the huts, and make other fixes.

One morning, as Odell was cleaning her bow at the rear of her hut, Marcus and Maximus appeared.

"Odell, Marcus and I were wondering whether you would be good enough to guide us back to where you found us; we left behind tools, which would be useful to help fix up the settlement."

"Also, we've left a few coins and pieces of jewellery behind. We thought these might allow you to buy essentials at the local market." Said Marcus.

Odell lifted her head slightly, but stayed silent to consider their proposition.

"I'll make a deal with you, I'll take you to that place on two conditions, the first, you tell me what you were doing in the forest when I found you and second, you help me with the daily hunt for food."

"Done," said Maximus. "We are engineers sent to the forest to build a road to the port at the entrance to the estuary. The road is to aid the movement of wood and iron ore, but also soldiers to fight on the Welsh border."

"Why is Wales so important to the Romans?" asked Odell.

"It's prized for its minerals, especially its copper and gold." Said Marcus.

"Understood, there is something else I want to ask you both," said Odell, looking serious. "I've noticed Freya and one of your men, the young Julius, have struck up a friendship. Is he trustworthy? I don't want him leading her on. She's only just found her voice and whilst it makes me happy to see him helping her with her chores, I don't want her led astray. Also, I don't want her falling for someone who is going to leave, understood?"

"Yes. He is a good man, but I will have a discreet word with him if that would make you feel better?" Said Maximus.

Odell nodded.

It didn't take long for the men to be accepted by most of the settlement. Ma, however, proved harder to crack, she kept herself to herself and rarely spoke to the men unless it was to scold them.

Early one freezing January morning, Odell roused Maximus and Marcus from their warm beds. A harsh wind swirled around the settlement, stinging their faces. Although there was no hoar frost, the ground was rock hard underfoot. They set off into the forest with the old grey horse and four hunting dogs, after half an hour, they came to a halt, Odell set the dogs loose, they immediately dashed off to the north of the tree line.

"What happens now?" Asked Marcus.

"We wait." Replied Odell. But it wasn't long before the urgent baying of the dogs filled the air.

"I think they've got one," said Odell, jumping up and running in the direction of the ruckus. Marcus and Maximus followed, but Odell ran like the wind and by the time they caught up, she had already dispatched a young boar with her hunting spear. No sooner was it trussed, ready for the sledge, then the hounds caught the scent of further prey and roared off in pursuit. The second pig was far bigger and took several attempts to fell.

"Good work Odell," said Marcus, grinning widely.

"Yes, we shall eat well tonight." Came her reply.

"What about our tools and other belongings?" asked Maximus.

"They are just over that ridge ahead, gather what you need, I will stay here."

The two men strode off, but curious, Odell tied up the horse and dogs and followed. Peeping over the ridgeline, she saw the two soldiers below, they moved towards a rocky outcrop, they seemed to remove several heavy stones. They then leant into a dip or hole in the ground to remove a few items, chatting animatedly as they did so. A short time later, they returned with leather bags strung across their bodies.

That night everyone ate together in the long hut, the central cooking fire filled the space with warm light, a sense of well-being imbrued the air. They ate hungrily, tearing large chunks of meat from the bone, washed down with homebrewed beer. After everyone had eaten, they took turns telling stories. Odell sat to the side of the group and surveyed the scene. Alwin had grown close to Marcus, so much so, he barely left his side and other friendships were blossoming. Ma, on the other hand, was still sulking, Odell hoped given time, she might soften her stance.

A week later, Marcus, Maximus and Odell were once again in the forest searching for food, they had taken a path by the ponds and were in a hollow looking for signs of recent deer activity. Without warning Odell jumped up, she turned her head to one side, a frown crossed her features, placing her right index finger to her lips she gesticulated to the two soldiers to move off the track and take cover under the thick, low branches of an ancient fir tree.

"Do not, under any circumstances, show yourselves." She instructed in an urgent whisper; it was only then Marcus and Maximus heard the thunder of hooves approaching. Odell stood tall, with hands-on-hips as the horses rounded the corner.

"Look Alfred, it's your feisty cousin," shouted Edgar, who was the lead horseman,

he pulled his horse up abruptly.

"Alfred, it's your obnoxious sidekick," replied Odell, pulling a face.

"Cousin, good to see you," said a laughing Alfred. "What brings you to this part of the forest?"

"I should ask you the same?"

"We are here to seek filthy Romans," said Edgar, with his jaw clenched.

"Same old, same old," replied Odell, feigning a yawn.

Alfred urged his horse towards her. "We've heard there are Romans in this part of the forest, that they are being sheltered by locals, we are going to seek them out and kill them all." Alfred's face was red and sweaty.

"There are no Romans, I don't know where you got your information from but it's farcical. Don't you think I would know if they were here?" Said Odell shaking her head.

"I, for one, don't trust you, you're always so condescending towards us." Spat Edgar.

"No, only you Edgar, now be on your way, I have prey to kill."

"You need to be taught a lesson, the firm strap of a man you shameless hag."

"Enough, Edgar! Good to see you cousin, may your hunting be productive." Said Alfred as he spurred his horse forward into a trot, soon the sound of hooves had disappeared, and Marcus and Maximus emerged from their hiding place.

"Odell, do you have a death wish?" Asked a frowning Maximus.

"I'd say, you were remarkable, brave and defiant." Said Marcus through a wide grin.

"Thank you, but we need to be extra careful from now on. I know my cousin and he's like a dog with a bone, he will not stop looking for you. So, we will need to outwit him and his men, which shouldn't be too taxing." Odell broke into a giggle as she said this.

"You would do well not to underestimate Edgar's hostility towards you though." Said Maximus.

"Edgar is a contemptuous fool."

"That may be so, but Maximus is right, don't drop your guard, I sense he's a danger to you." Odell shot the two men a look, before turning and climbing a grassy slope.

It was dusk when they returned to the settlement, Alwin was at the gate to greet them. Odell took one look at his expectant face and knew that something was up, but before he could warn her, Ma appeared.

"I told you no good would come of this, I told you not to let these scum into our lives." She screamed at the top of her voice.

It was as much as Odell could do to concentrate on Ma's words, for her grandmother was such a sight, face red and contorted, arms waving furiously in the cold air.

"Ma, calm down a minute, whatever has happened?" Asked Odell.

"One of those bastards has been stealing our belongings and selling them at the local market for profit. Almost all our grain store has gone, not to mention many belongings, wiped out by a thieving Roman and if that wasn't enough, he's taken your mother's brooch, It's the only thing I had left of her!" tears streamed down Ma's cheeks as she dropped to her knees, sobbing."

"Who? Which man has done this?" Asked Marcus, picking Ma up in his arms.

Ma made a feeble attempt to resist before she buried her head into his chest and allowed herself to be carried into her hut.

"Please Ma, tell me who has done this, and I promise, I will avenge you and your family." Said Marcus as he gently placed her on her bed.

"It's that thieving brute Tacitus who I kicked out a few minutes before you arrived." Ma's reply was tearful.

"We need to act fast before the rest of us are discovered, it must have been the locals at the market who told your cousin." Said Maximus.

"No! This is my responsibility. You will stay here and look after Ma; I will go. I know the terrain, plus I'm lighter and faster on foot than any of you." Not waiting for the dissent, she knew would follow, Odell ran off into the night, even in the blackness, she soon found Tacitus, it wasn't hard for such a seasoned hunter and besides, she could hear him flailing around in the undergrowth below.

An hour later, Odell returned to the settlement. Marcus and Maximus were still at Ma's side; they were eating some of the venison they had caught earlier. Odell walked across to her grandmother and placed a bag at her feet and an item in her hand, the missing brooch. A wide smile spread across Ma's face as she struggled to stand. Placing both hands either side of Odell's face, she kissed her granddaughter over and over.

"Thank you, thank you! You are my saviour. But what of the thief?"

CHAPTER 5

Present Day: Fairview Residential Home:

The task ahead did not daunt Harriet; indeed, she relished the challenge. It would keep her mind off Henry. No matter how hard she tried, he just kept creeping into her thoughts. She had spent the best part of the morning chatting with senior staff members, only to find each conversation ended the same way, if she wanted to gain an insight into Fairview and its residents, then there was only one person to ask, Ada Brown. It seemed, however, that this might prove trickier than first imagined, as General Manager Rita Pritchard was busy telling her in her prominent Glaswegian accent.

"Ada took to her room, following Major George Moore's death and is not receiving visitors. Indeed, our loud and energetic Ada has become monosyllabic and depressed. At present, we are at a loss for how to help her."

"Poor Ada, grief is such a complicated matter; in my experience, everyone deals with it differently. Whilst I have no wish to add to her distress, I would really like to speak to her." Said Harriet.

"Well, we can try, but don't get your hopes up." Rita rose from her desk and moved towards the door; Harriet dutifully followed down the impressive entrance hall and up a sweeping stone staircase, along a carpeted corridor, until Rita came to a large, heavy door on the third floor. Rita knocked loudly, and the two women entered. It was a large light room with a high ceiling, beautifully decorated in pastel tones and stylishly furnished. On the opposite side of the room, a seated figure was looking out of a window.

"Ada, what are you doing, dear? I have a visitor for you."

"I'm waiting to die, Rita."

"Oh, don't, Ada, please don't say that. I've brought someone to see you."

"I said no visitors, Rita."

"But it might help."

"Help me die?"

"Ada, stop this nonsense now, you don't mean it."

"But you see Rita, I do, I'm sitting here waiting to die."

"What if I were to tell you this visitor needs your help?"

"Still no."

"She's a police officer who wants to find out what happened to George. Her name is Harriet..." before Rita could finish, Ada spun her wheelchair around and made her way towards Harriet with alarming speed, screeching to a halt only when she was within touching distance. Ada took hold of the glasses hanging around her neck and leant into scrutinise the woman in the smart blue dress and jacket.

"You are too beautiful to be a police officer, that face of yours must have got you unwanted attention over the years." Somewhat taken aback, Harriet did not reply.

"I'm sorry, Rita, but I am not receiving guests today, or tomorrow, or next week."

"Ada, I completely understand. I'm so sorry for your loss." Said Harriet. Rita shrugged her shoulders and gestured to Harriet to follow her.

It was several days before Harriet tried again, but Ada was not in the least bit interested in engaging. Then one morning less than a week later while Harriet was interviewing a member of staff, Ada's carer Linda, knocked on the door to the library and brought Harriet a handwritten note, it simply said, *"I will see you at 3.pm."*

At the appointed time Harriet entered Ada's room as always, accompanied by Rita Pritchard, Ada was seated in the wheelchair, with her back to them staring at something outside, as she had been, the first time Harriet visited.

"What I want to know young lady, is whether you are any good? Is it going to be worth my while speaking to you?"

Harriet walked across and knelt beside the old lady, taking one of her tiny hands in hers. "I like to think that I am a methodical officer, I am not easily put off, I am determined, even tenacious. I will try my best to be the police officer you need me to be."

Ada burst out laughing, "in that case, I think we may be able to work together."

"I look forward to it," said Harriet, glancing at an open-mouthed Rita Pritchard.

"Rita, darling, is there any chance of some sandwiches? Harriet and I will be having a working afternoon tea today." Ada winked at Harriet.

Rita rolled her eyes before walking towards the door.

What a character Ada was, intelligent, compelling, and mischievous, Harriet liked her already.

Ada studied the young woman watching Rita leave the room. There was something about her, but it was too early to say what.

To Harriet's surprise, Ada leapt out of the wheelchair and took a seat at a rather lovely round wooden table in the centre of the room, she beckoned to Harriet to join her.

"I don't need the wheelchair, it was George's, but I found some comfort in sitting in it."

"Ada, you are full of surprises," said Harriet before continuing, "I need your help to find out what has been going on at Fairview, everyone I've spoken to tells me you are the person to ask. "

"Well, I suppose I am invariably at the centre of everything, I love people, I love to be with people. I've made it my business to get to know everyone."

"Then you are very much the woman for this job. Now, if you don't mind, I'd like to run through my questions in order?"

"Fire away, young lady."

"How well do you know Eileen Graham?"

"I know her well, when I first moved here near enough five years ago, she was lucid, she'd just been diagnosed with dementia and was finding it difficult to cope with the diagnosis. She had a great sense of humour, and we used to enjoy afternoon tea together two or three times a week. But as time passed, she became more and more reclusive, and latterly verbally abusive. Do you know much about dementia, Harriet?"

"I know a little, I lost my father to it not so long ago. It's a terrible illness, it robs the individual of their memories and their sense of self, and family and friends of their loved one, it's truly heart-breaking."

"You are right, even though treatment for dementia patients has improved in the last few years here at Fairview, the high turnover of staff has affected Eileen deeply. She needs consistency, for a while, there was a lack of stability, and she became more verbally abusive and sometimes physically violent. I put this down to the frustration she felt at not being able to communicate effectively with others, not being able to concentrate on conversations. She is frail, yes, but sometimes she needs to be restrained for her own safety. During a conversation we had last year when she was cogent, I recall her telling me of a rage burning inside her at the injustice of her condition and sometimes she couldn't control it, it just spilt out."

"Would you say with your knowledge of her, she's capable of making a complaint?"

"Well, here's the thing: dementia is a complex condition, there are times of lucidity, but, in my experience, the frequency of this slows until it just doesn't happen anymore. I would say potentially, but I wouldn't like to say for sure."

"That's fair enough and helpful, Ada. You seem to know a lot about the subject, has dementia touched your life?"

"I suppose it has, I used to work with clients with symptoms."

"Gosh, do you mind my asking in what capacity?"

"I ran a shelter for women who had experienced domestic violence." A frown flitted across her face. Harriet noticed Ada spoke deliberately and did not use the usual phrase 'domestic violence victims', but before she could ask more about her past work, there was a knock, and a grinning Mike Taylor popped his head around the door.

"Ladies, sorry to interrupt but Harriet, we have a four-thirty meeting with Stanley Cross in the Library."

"So, we do, I'm sorry Ada, this is my colleague Mike, and he's right, I must go. May I come and see you again tomorrow.?"

"Only if you bring that lovely young man with you for a cup of tea." Said Ada, winking at Mike. Harriet and Mike exchanged grins.

Stanley Cross was waiting for them in the green lounge. Harriet could tell he was a tall man, for he was sitting with his legs outstretched and they seemed to go on forever. He was thin, but well turned out, with short white hair and a moustache. He was wearing a shirt and tie with a knitted mustard waistcoat. The meeting was difficult; despite their best efforts, neither of them could get Stanley to talk.

The following afternoon, around three, Harriet knocked on Ada's door and waited for a response.

"If that's you Harriet, you may enter, but only if you have that lovely young man in tow."

It was a widely smiling Harriet who entered. Mike followed on behind.

What they found was unexpected; Ada's round walnut table was set for afternoon tea. There were teacups and saucers and porcelain tea plates, dainty little sandwiches, and a variety of cupcakes. Sat next to Ada was Stanley Cross in a smart crimson waistcoat.

"Come in, come in, join us, and tuck in," said Ada through a mouthful of sandwich. "I understand from Stanley yesterday's meeting was futile. Stanley, and I have had a chat and we have a proposition to put to you." Ada smiled at Stanley.

"We would appreciate any help you can give us." Said Mike, Harriet nodded.

"Good, then I will get to the point. Stanley is a lovely man who just cannot bring himself to, let's say, verbally implicate anyone in wrongdoing. But he has a relative who's a gold digger." Harriet noticed Stanley shoot Ada a look.

"Sorry Stanley, but it's true and you know it. Anyway, where was I? Oh yes, Stanley will permit you to put a covert camera in his room so you can see for yourselves." Stanley's eyes filled with tears; Ada squeezed his hand.

"Oh, my goodness Stanley, please don't be upset; we just want to help." Said Harriet, leaning in towards him.

"I know, and I want it to stop, but it's so painful and besides, it's already too late. I've no money left, no assets." Stanley stared at his plate, his bottom lip quivering. "I shall have to leave my home here and my friends and live out the rest of my days; I know not where." Stanley produced a large white handkerchief from his pocket and blew his nose noisily.

"Nonsense Stanley, I assure you the next time you leave Fairview, it will be in a coffin a long time from now. I have already told you; your place here is secure, you can stay for as long as you like." Ada folded her arms across her chest.

"But how is that possible? My bank accounts are almost empty. I can no longer pay for my keep."

"All I'm at liberty to say is that an anonymous benefactor has come forward. You are too important a part of the community to lose. And, anyway, this patron won't take no for an answer." An enormous smile spread across Stanley's face.

"Well, thank you, Stanley, Sergeant Lacey, and I will discuss the covert camera with our boss, Derek Wynn, and report back. There's one other thing, would you be prepared to sign some paperwork to allow us access your bank accounts?" said Mike gently.

Stanley nodded vigorously, unable to speak due to the volume of cake he'd just crammed into his mouth.

"Before you two go, there is something else that might be of interest, you remember we were talking about Eileen Graham yesterday, Harriet?" She nodded. "Well, I mentioned her to Stanley, and he recalls an incident with her about three weeks ago. Stanley?"

"Yes, well, Eileen and I were pottering around the garden, arm in arm in the spring sunshine, when she suddenly came to a standstill, turned to me, and said, "no cocoa, no cocoa." Her face was white and her eyes wide open, I was concerned, and I tried to get her to say more, but she had already drifted back into a confused state."

"Any idea what she meant by that?" asked Harriet.

"I've thought and thought about it and both Ada and I now think she might have been referring to the nightly cocoa round managed by Ethel Moore."

"Who's she?" asked Mike.

"Ethel is a member of staff, she's in her early sixties and lives on site. Her job is to provide bedtime cocoa and be 'on call' during the night should any of the Residents require anything." Said Ada.

"Like what sort of thing? And is she well-liked?" Asked Harriet.

"Drinks, a sandwich, an additional blanket, company, and I would say not particularly, she's quite rude and insensitive. She's alright if you do as she asks, but if not, she can be abrasive." Ada pulled a face.

"Stanley?" Asked Harriet.

"I agree, she also seems to spend an inordinate amount of time asleep. Good luck trying to get her to respond to you during the night."

The following day, Derek Wynn called a meeting to catch up with the team and establish what progress if any they'd made with their allocated lines of enquiry.

"Thank you all for making the effort to come in early this morning, I'm keen to see how we are getting on," Derek took a sip of coffee, "let's start with Eileen Graham, Paul and Steven, did you find anything significant on the photos of the bruising?"

"Our examination of the photos provided by Mr and Mrs Graham confirmed a hand made the bruising, with sufficient force to produce a considerable rupturing of blood vessels and capillaries under the skin on the wrists." Said, Paul Jones.

"But, to move this forward, we contacted Mr and Mrs Graham and Rita Pritchard and gained permission to visit Eileen and to photograph both arms with reflective ultraviolet photography. Even though there were no longer bruises visible to the naked eye, we were able to get some significant results." Steven held up a couple of photos, which clearly showed extensive bruising to Eileen's forearms and her wrists.

"Long-wave UV light penetrates deeper into the skin than visible light and so the film will pick up the image of a bruise which has been absorbed deep into the skin." Said, Paul.

"That's right, but we also made another more significant discovery," Steven held up a third photo, gasps reverberated around the room.

"This bite mark to the right forearm went deep into the tissue, it provides sufficient detail to be able to compare it to the bite of any suspect that may emerge." Said, Paul.

"This is brilliant work, you two, taken all together, this suggests Eileen is the victim of assault. I need to speak to Rita Pritchard about additional safety measures while we continue to investigate. Does anyone else have anything to add before we move on?" asked Derek.

"There is something Sir, it might be nothing, but whilst Harriet and I were talking to Stanley Cross yesterday, he told us in a rare moment of lucidity, and out of the blue, Eileen became distressed and said and I quote, "no cocoa, no cocoa." It appears there's a member of staff who provides residents with cocoa at bedtime." Said Mike.

"I'd like you both to speak to this staff member, just gently probe, see if anything comes out of this, please." Derek made a note in his policy document. "Now, let's talk about Stanley Cross, Mike and Harriet?"

Harriet had just finished explaining their unexpected encounter with Ada and Stanley the day before, when there was a knock at the door and Kate Squires popped into the room.

"I'm very sorry to be so late, I've had quite a morning of it." She entered the briefing room, holding a small cardboard box in her right hand.

"Harriet, this is for you, it came by taxi about an hour ago. Reception tried to get hold of Paul, but apparently, deemed me an acceptable alternative. I decided it might be prudent to treat it with caution, bearing in mind past less pleasant packages, in particular the live snake! However, after a cursory examination, I'm pretty sure it doesn't pose a threat to anyone in its current form." Kate handed the box to Harriet, who peered inside and lifted out a white mug covered in clingfilm. Placing it down, she unfolded a note, a huge grin spread across her face.

"Come on, let us out of our misery, what's this all about?" asked Derek Wynn.

"I'll read it to you."

"Harriet dear, Stanley's account of Eileen's outburst troubled me and, as usual, sleep did not come easy last night. I, therefore, carried out some detective work. At 2.am this morning, I let myself into the main kitchen. Using my trusty torch, I was able to locate the Cocoa trolley and, as I suspected, Ethel had been too lazy to clear it following her round, leaving it instead for the morning kitchen staff. What you have in the box is a surplus mug of cocoa for analysis, good luck and I look forward to our next chat. Yours, Ada."

"What an extraordinary woman." Said Derek.

"Oh, you don't know the half of it, she is astonishing."

"And amusing." Said Mike, interrupting Harriet.

"Yes, indeed." Harriet put the note down and was about to put the mug back in the box when Paul Jones walked across and took it from her.

"I don't know why, it's just a feeling, but I think we should analyse its contents, seeing as Ada has gone to such trouble, and because I have news regarding the death of Vera Mortimer."

"Yes, do it, never let it be said that we didn't pursue every avenue. And you have? Well, tell us." Said Derek.

"I attended the post-mortem as requested, it was straightforward, there were no obvious signs of foul play, nothing to alarm the pathologist. They took the usual samples for analysis and that's what I want to talk about. Vera's stomach contained traces of undigested cocoa, I checked, drinks are served at Fairview between 9.30 and 10 pm each evening. Total emptying of the stomach occurs between four and five hours after consumption, so, if Vera drank the cocoa at about 10.pm, it would be reasonable to assume she died sometime between 10 pm and 3 am. The contents of her stomach suggest it was more likely between 1 am and 2 am. In both her stomach contents and blood samples, Fentanyl, a potent opioid painkiller, was present, but the blood sample contained an alarmingly high dose. High doses can cause someone to become extremely sleepy and their breathing can be affected. Extremely high doses can lead to death. So, subject to there being no other contradictory evidence, this is now a suspicious death. What we don't yet know is whether Vera took the drug deliberately, or mistakenly, or if it was administered to her by someone? The lab is currently carrying out further tests and I've asked the Pathologist to take another look at Vera's body. She ingested fentanyl, yet it's not clear if it was in sufficient quantity to kill her. I want to know how such high concentrations ended up in her system."

"Blimey, good work Paul, this is significant, it would seem to tie in with the phone calls received by the CQC from the female staff member who alleged the systematic overmedicating of patients. I need to think about our next move. Please update me as soon as you have anything." Said Derek.

"Okay, where were we? Ah yes, let's go back to Stanley Cross for a moment, shall we? Kate and Steven, anything significant in the footage provided by his daughter, Sharon Dean?"

"Well, yes, and no, what I mean is the quality is poor. However, it looks as if the individual in the images is a woman wearing one of Fairview's royal blue staff uniforms, worn by all personal carers." Said Kate.

"Can I just ask how you think it's a woman? If I recollect, only the lower half of the body is visible?" Asked Derek.

"Well, Sir, not to put too fine a point on it, it's the shape of the individual's rear!" said Steven, breaking into a smile.

"Okay, I walked into that one."

"The uniform is like hospital scrubs; a tunic worn over trousers, but in this case, the trousers are a poor fit, they are very short. We've identified what looks like a tattoo on the left ankle, we are currently attempting to get the image enhanced." Said Kate.

"Good work, you two, with Mike and Harriet's breakthrough regarding the covert camera and access to Stanley's bank accounts, we should be able to progress this. "

"I'm pretty sure Ada Brown knows who's been stealing from Stanley," said Mike.

"Undoubtedly, she said as much, I think it will turn out to be Sharon Dean," said Harriet.

"Why would she risk involving the police and why provide footage?" Asked Derek.

"She's drained Stanley's accounts; she needs another source of income. I think she thinks she can have one over on us all, as I've said previously, I think she may be planning to take legal action against Fairview for failing to protect her father from an abusive member of staff, all bogus, of course." Said Mike.

"I agree," said Harriet; "we need to find out if Sharon has a tattoo on her left ankle."

"Finally, Steven, and Harriet, any progress regarding the death of Major George Moore?" asked Derek.

"The post-mortem is due towards the end of the week; I hope to know more then." Said, Steven.

"I haven't yet had the chance to talk to Ada about this, it will be my priority tomorrow." Harriet replied.

Harriet had just entered Ada's room when her mobile burst into life, she gestured to Ada she needed to take the call and left the room.

"Harriet, it's Paul Jones. I wanted to let you know as soon as possible; the results are back from the mug of cocoa."

"And?"

"It does indeed contain fentanyl, ground-up tablets, to be exact. The sample did not contain enough to kill, but sufficient to induce sleep."

"Well done, Ada."

"Yes, indeed, you don't suppose Ada could be in danger, do you?"

"What do you mean, Paul?"

"Well, she's been snooping around. Surely she must have been noticed?"

"I see what you mean."

"Are you going to tell her?" asked Paul. Harriet did not reply immediately; "I'm going to have to think about it."

CHAPTER 6

408 AD Gloucestershire:

Ma asked again, "what of the thief?"

Odell turned to Maximus and Marcus and slowly drew her index finger across her throat.

"I would have returned with him had he not tried to force himself upon me. But when he unbuttoned himself and tried to grab me, I knew there would be a fight." Odell shrugged.

"Are you harmed?" asked a frowning Marcus.

"No, the only injury is to my clothing, look it's torn." Odell fingered her tunic.

"What I need now is a drink, preferably a strong one."

Ma laughed as she poured a large measure of Mead.

Odell threw the sweet sticky liquid down in one before wiping her mouth clean with her sleeve. "That's better, thanks Ma."

A few days later, Marcus and Odell found themselves alone. An old tree trunk provided a welcome seat as they waited for the hunting dogs to summon them. The spring sunshine penetrated the thick foliage to provide a little warmth and bluebells carpeted the forest floor; their intoxicating fragrance scenting the air.

"Marcus, tell me a bit about yourself. I don't believe I even know what land you were born in," said Odell.

"I was born in a land called Abyssinia, a world away from here. My family farmed and hunted on land just outside the capital Aksum, which lies nearly a hundred miles from the sea the Romans call Pontus Herculis (sea of Hercules)."

"What does it look like?"

"It has mountains and forests and rivers, but also large plains, and the climate can be extremely hot."

"I see, so tell me, how was it you ended up here?"

"It's a long story, but essentially, a slave trader called Felix Augusta seized me when I was a young boy, I believe I was seven, I was on my way to market, but never made it. I was taken by caravan to the coast and put on a ship." Odell noticed Marcus touched his choker as he spoke, a black leather string from which a large tooth hung.

"That must have been tough for you and frightening. Is that choker from your homeland?"

"It is all I have left of that life; my father gave it to me shortly before I was abducted. This is the tooth of a lion; it represents courage and bravery."

"But how did you end up as a Gladiator?"

"I was taken to Rome, the capital, and sold to a man called Quintus Agricola, who owned the famous Ludus Magnus Gladiator training school. He was a fair man. I was well looked after, put to work cleaning up after the Gladiators, household tasks, mainly. As I grew, I moved onto repairing and cleaning their weapons, knives, swords, shields, and helmets. It took me a while to learn the native tongue. I went onto learn several other languages through my contact with the fighters. I now speak a little Greek, a little Gaul and, of course, your tongue."

"You have led such an unusual life, full of challenge, it makes mine seem insignificant in comparison."

"Not at all, I am in awe of the way you have taken on the role of leader at such a young age. Your people would have died long ago without you, I can see that every single day is a struggle for survival." Odell and Marcus locked eyes, for an instant.

"But you still haven't told me how you ended up in the Gladiator ring?" Said Odell. Marcus grinned before answering. "I grew from a skinny young boy into a tall, muscular young man. This did not go unnoticed by master Quintus, who entered me in the training programme. As it happens, I took to it and became quite good with the sword and spear, Quintus entered me into competitions."

"Just how good did you become?"

"He was exceptional, one of the best Gladiators in Rome." said a smiling Maximus as he wandered across with a brace of wild duck in his hands.

"Thank you, my friend, but I'm not sure that's quite accurate."

"It absolutely is, you were so good you'd still be there if Quintus hadn't given you your freedom."

Marcus laughed loudly as he slapped a large hand on his friend's shoulder.

"How did you two meet?" asked Odell.

"We joined the army together, immediately hit it off." Said Maximus.

"I owe this man my life, I am indebted to him and will not leave his side until I have repaid him." Said a solemn Marcus.

"Tell me what happened, please?" Pleaded Odell.

"Do you really want to know?" asked Marcus, his eyebrows raised.

"Yes!"

"We were in the foothills of the eastern alps close to the Frigidus River, it was the autumn of 394 AD. We were fighting for Emperor Theodosius against the rebel army of Augustus Eugenius. We numbered well over 10,000 men, but it was a stormy afternoon and a harsh and bloody battle. Had it not been for Maximus, I and my century would have perished."

"Sorry, but what is a century?" Asked Odell.

"The Roman army comprises military units. A unit of four hundred and eighty soldiers is called a cohort, which is essentially six lots of eighty men, and these are called centuries."

"Understood. So what happened?"

"We found ourselves in a deep gully, with no way out, just as I prepared myself to die, I heard a commotion coming from the entrance to the gorge, as I wiped the blood and sweat from my eyes, I saw Maximus on horseback leading a cavalry charge towards us. I remember thinking I'd no idea he could ride! He scooped me up, and we turned around and cantered back through the enemy. Not only did he save me, but all my remaining men. So now you see why I am indebted to him."

"That's impressive, Maximus," said Odell.

"Marcus would have done the same for me. *Et honorem.*"

"E*t honorem,*" Marcus replied.

"What does that mean?" Asked Odell.

"Strength and honour," Maximus replied.

Against all her instincts, Odell had grown to like these two men, she would miss them. And she realised in that moment she no longer wanted them to leave.

Later, as they walked back to the settlement, Maximus sidled up to Odell, who was walking ahead.

"I need to talk to you; the time is coming when we shall have to determine our future."

Odell felt as if someone had punched her in the stomach, but said nothing.

"There is something, however, I must do before we decide which path to take. I wish to make the journey back to our garrison fortress at Corinium. I wish to speak to the Legate and find out why there's been no contact and to ascertain our new orders."

"Sorry Legate? What's that?"

"The senior commander."

"It will not be a straightforward journey, particularly with the likes of my cousin and his men in the vicinity. These are uncertain times; how do you intend to travel on horseback or by boat?"

"I'm not yet sure."

"As engineers, you and your men could build a boat. You could launch it from the bank at Noose (Modern name Awre) not too far from here but, the river is tidal. You would need to match your journey to the spring moon; it influences the tides which are extreme in this season. Alternatively, you will need horses; these are expensive, but would allow you to travel at greater speed through the forest and onwards to Glevum (Modern Gloucester). You could cross the river there and ride on to Corinium. But be under no illusion, the countryside is full of vagabonds who prey on travellers and are intent on capturing and killing Romans."

"I hear what you say, but I have no choice, I plan to take a Marcus and maybe a few men with me."

"You will need a guide, otherwise your odds will be terrible."

"As experienced soldiers, we will be fine."

"Exactly, you are roman soldiers, you stand out, which is the last thing required for such a mission."

"Okay, okay, I will give it some more thought."

A few days later, Maximus and Marcus went in search of Odell, they found her with Ma, sowing wheat. As they approached, Ma spotted them and nudged Odell, who turned around.

"I've given our chat the other day much thought, and I believe I've come up with a plan." Said Maximus.

"Go ahead," said Odell.

"It will take too long to build a boat, yes, we are capable, but time is of the essence. So, with your help, we will buy a couple of horses at the market, also, with your help, we will memorise the safest route. It will be Marcus and I who will make the journey, we estimate it will take us about a week."

"You two are more idiotic than I first thought," said Ma as Odell stifled a giggle, "as you know, I loathed you when you first arrived, but I have come to think highly of you and, in your case, Marcus, I think of you like a son. Your plan stinks, it will result in certain failure and probable death." Maximus stood with his mouth ajar.

"Ma is right, your plan is doomed to failure. For a start, buying two horses at the local market will generate suspicion because of their value, we will need to go further afield. You will need someone local with you to advise on the best route, depending on the circumstances at the time."

Maximus looked at the ground, Marcus paced up and down.

"Is there someone from the settlement who'd be prepared to act as our guide and mentor?" asked Marcus.

"Maybe."

"No, I forbid it, Odell, it's too dangerous." Shouted Ma. Odell held up her palm to her grandmother.

"If Maximus is determined to go, I will accompany him, but only on the condition, Marcus stays behind to look after Ma and the settlement."

"No," said Maximus.

"No," said Marcus.

"Yes," said Ma.

"Take it or leave it." Odell turned back and continued to sow as before.

A week later, Odell and Maximus left the settlement for Corinium dressed as traders, they carried a selection of pottery items with them for continuity. To begin with, they walked on foot, leading the horses through the forest to the river. They followed the riverbank until they reached a small settlement known as Blakeney, then on to the tiny settlement of Westbury, where they encountered steep ground and were forced to ride further inland, until they were once more able to access the riverbank. They pushed on until dusk, when Odell spotted a wooded hillock to their left; she gestured to Maximus to make in that direction. They would camp there for the night, Odell guessed they were within three miles of Glevum, she had never been so far from home. Their camp, however, provided a good vantage point, they could see for miles in every direction. Confident there was no one in their vicinity, they made camp and lit a small fire; they ate a rabbit skilfully snared by Odell on the south slope.

"Odell, do you have any plans or hopes for the future?" Maximus asked from underneath his blanket.

"I'm not sure what you mean?" Came her reply.

"Well, is there anything you want to achieve? Any place you want to travel?"

"To be honest, I've never had time to think of such things. My life has been about survival, I live from day to day."

"But do you have a passion for anything?"

Odell didn't immediately reply for, she was thinking.

"I'm a good hunter, one might say I have a passion for the forest, I love it, it lifts my spirits; I love to run through the trees and pit myself against the elements."

"Do you ever wish for a family for yourself?"

"I'm not sure the gods have that in mind for me. I shall continue doing what I do and see where it leads."

"Good response," said Maximus yawning, for it had been a long day.

In the morning, they lit a fire and cooked porridge, once they'd breakfasted, they packed up the camp. It was shortly after dawn when they set off on their journey once more; it did not take long to reach the river bridge at Glevum. The noise, people everywhere buying, selling, shouting, laughing, arguing, and crying, took Odell aback. Animals, sheep, cows, chickens roamed in the mud and effluence which squelched underfoot. The stench of overcrowding was impossible to escape, it burned into her nostrils. They dismounted and led their horses, Odell tried to keep close to Maximus, bewildered by the scene before her. Dark figures ran in and out of the shadows, Odell perspired, sensing her discomfort, Maximus stopped and waited for her to catch up.

"It's okay, stay close to me, we will soon reach the countryside again." He said, smiling. He led them away from the market towards the dockside, here, Odell saw many wooden boats loading and unloading, the boat crews were a colourful mixture of individuals, some from far-flung places. What she didn't see were Roman soldiers. They exited the docks to find themselves on the outskirts of the settlement, a short time later, they were back in the countryside.

"Why did you not go to the Roman Fort at Glevum?" Asked Odell.

"Because it has not been operational for many, many, years, the fort and settlement became a Colonia, which is a self-governing Roman city for retired soldiers, their partners and families."

"Are you telling me that soldiers stayed here and took local women as lovers and had families with them?" Odell raised her eyebrows.

"Yes, many of the soldiers did not return home to their wives and families, but stayed and made lives for themselves here." Odell shook her head several times. Over the last day or so, her knowledge of the world had widened immeasurably.

It took them another two and a half days to reach the outskirts of Corinium. Along the way, they passed vast and opulent roman villas, as well as many small farms and settlements. Odell could not shake a deep sense of unease. She was sure they were being observed indeed that they had been since leaving Glevum, but she kept these thoughts and feelings to herself, for she had no proof.

When they were about half a mile from Corinium, Maximus came to a halt.

"Odell, I need to prepare you for what you will see at Corinium. Glevum is a large lively settlement, but Corinium is vast in comparison. If you like, I can leave you here while I go in search of the fort commander. I will come back for you, I promise."

"No, I go where you go, no matter what." Odell planted her hands on her hips.

"Alright, as long as you are sure?" Odell did not budge.

"Before we go on, I want you to know the truth about Marcus and I. They stationed us at Caerleon (near Newport Wales) as part of the Second Augustian Legion, consisting of 5,000 men. But then orders came for our cohort to travel to Corinium, it took us several weeks to reach the fort. On arrival, we found it had a new commander, Julius Maximus. He swore us to secrecy and told us our orders came directly from the new emperor, Flavius Claudius Constantinus, a roman general who had just seized power in the western roman territory. He is currently in Gaul. We were told to march into the wooded Dobunni tribal territory and build a road parallel to the river with the upmost speed. It was to be used to transport minerals and coal across the water to Gaul, to help pay for the emperor's conquest but, also to transport hundreds of Roman soldiers not to fight across the border in Cambria (Wales) as I told you before, but to help to quash increasing resistance over the water. After several weeks of work, our supplies dried up and bad weather set in. The rest, you know, I need to find out why they left us behind."

"I'm still coming with you."

Despite Maximus's warnings about the size of Corinium, Odell could not help but issue an involuntary gasp as they rode through a vast stone gateway into the city. Row upon row of wooden buildings were set on straight roads in a grid pattern. Houses, shops, workshops, animal shelters and more. They rode down the central highway as townsfolk milled around them. There were people as far as the eye could see, dogs barking, children running in the filth of town life, men yelling, women screeching. Townsfolk jostled and barged their way past them. After some time, Odell did not know how long, they left the madness behind. In the foreground, a stone wall towered above the roof line. Maximus came to a halt and dismounted, Odell did the same, leading her horse, she followed Maximus through an enormous gateway, the gatehouse was unguarded. Odell could see the fort was rectangular, surrounded by a soaring stone wall and an earthen rampart, there were a series of internal towers set into the wall, she could count four gates to the stronghold. It was completely out of her realm of experience; she stood open-mouthed for a minute or two until Maximus called to her and beckoned her to follow him.

"Where are we heading?" She gasped.

"To the Principia, the administrative centre."

Every building they came across was unoccupied, empty, the commander's residence, the hospital, the workshops, the granary, storerooms, and barracks. It looked like Julius Maximus and his men had left with some haste, for there were the tell-tale signs of half-eaten meals in the refectory and abandoned possessions.

"I just don't understand what's happened here, it makes little sense." Said Maximus.

"Left in a hurry, they did, rumour has it the emperor ordered all able-bodied men to Gaul as a matter of urgency." Said an old man sitting on the ground with his back against the wall of the hospital.

"How do you know?" asked Maximus.

"Cos, me and my family run the tavern just outside the gate and men with beer in their bellies talk freely." The man pointed to a building just visible outside the main entrance, and, as if to emphasise his point, at that very moment, a group of noisy men fell out of the tavern door into the spring sunshine.

"Thank you." Said Maximus, bowing to the man who simply shrugged.

Maximus looked glum; his shoulders sloped as he stared at the cobbles underfoot.

They walked back through the city in silence, only when they reached

the outskirts of the town did they mount their steeds. Maximus rode fast, it

was all Odell could do to keep up, but she said nothing, by mid-afternoon, they

reached a small, wooded area.

"We'll camp here for the night." Said Maximus.

"I don't like it. It's too open."

"We camp here."

Odell shrugged, taking her bow, she walked off towards a little brook.

Maximus would have to build the campfire tonight, they needed to eat; they'd

had nothing since breakfast. Troubled by Maximus's poor mood, she missed

the first sign they had company, then she heard a cry and the crunch of twigs

breaking underfoot. She ran for the cover of a nearby tree before carefully and

silently doubling back, by keeping low, plentiful bracken hid her presence. As

she turned a corner, she saw four men, two holding their horses, one rifling

through their saddlebags, the fourth, a large heavy man, had Maximus pinned

up against a tree with a knife to his throat. She watched as he punched

Maximus in the face, he did not react, then a second punch. Why, she

wondered was he not fighting back? An argument broke out between the

group, Odell used this as the opportunity to get closer, the heavy-set man was

ugly, a bulbus red nose dominated his dirty face, he had tiny weasel like eyes.

He was unkempt, matted long hair and beard and he smelt so bad it filled her nostrils, a pungent stink, even though she was some distance away.

"Why the 'Feck' won't you tell us where your travelling companion is?" Asked the big man. Maximus did not respond, so the man punched him again.

"Anything of value?" Shouted the assailant to the others.

"A few bits and pieces, and the horses of course," came the response from one of the others.

Odell had seen enough, taking her bow, she armed it and aimed, the first arrow flew at speed finding its target with ease, a high-pitched squeal emanated from the man rifling through their belongings, then a second shriek and a third. All three men had been shot in the leg. Odell walked into the open, Maximus looked at her wide-eyed, a sheen of sweat covering his features. The large man immediately grabbed Maximus and placed his knife to his neck once more, but still Odell kept coming, her bow fully drawn.

"Don't, leave, save yourself." Shouted Maximus.

"Aww, what do we have here then, a lovely slip of a girl, you will do nicely, I bet you taste good! I'm going to have you once I've finished this coward off." The man whistled and made lecherous gestures towards Odell.

Odell spat in the man's direction, he laughed loudly, but clearly his intentions had struck a nerve with Maximus, for finally, his nostrils flared, and his eyes were full of menace.

Odell ran full pelt towards the man, at the last minute she dropped her bow and took her hunting knife from her belt, she threw herself at him, stabbing him in the neck before bouncing off his torso and running out of arms reach. He howled in pain as he grabbed his neck with large, chapped hands. Maximus was on his feet now; he ran to a pile of their belongings thrown to the ground by the vagabonds and retrieved his sword.

With sword in hand, Maximus rushed at the large man, he swung at him the steel blade landed on the man's left arm, howling in pain, the man, red with rage, ran after Maximus. Lurching forward, he caught the back of Maximus's foot, knocking him to the floor, before hurling himself on top, they fought ferociously, but Maximus was younger, lighter, and defter. Still, despite several sword blows, the man did not yield. Meanwhile, one of the three men injured by Odell was on his feet and limping towards the fighting men, Odell ran at him and kicked him in the face, this decked him, it was only then she noticed the other two were attempting to flee with their horses. She could not let this happen and ran back to her discarded bow, two perfect shots dismounted the men, both of whom thudded to the ground. They went quiet, satisfied they would cause no immediate trouble; Odell ran back towards Maximus, the large man was now on his feet with his back to her, Odell ran at him, she jumped up and grabbed him around the neck. Although small, she was strong and held on tight, using her legs to kick him in the ribs, eventually, he broke free, and in doing so Odell fell to the ground, striking her head on a rock, within seconds, darkness flooded over her.

CHAPTER 7

Present Day: Fairview Residential Home:

Harriet's telephone call ended and she re-entered Ada Browns bedroom. Ada was busy popping sugar cubes into her mouth.

"Sorry, Ada, but I had to take that call, now where were we? Ah yes, the cup of cocoa. You are one of the most clever and dogged individuals I have ever met, full of surprises."

"Oh, shut up and pour yourself a cup of tea." Ada was smiling. Not put off, Harriet continued, "thanks to you, our enquiries are accelerating, it was brilliant, you will forgive me if I don't go into detail just yet, I need to be careful what I say and its early days."

"Of course, dear, happy to be of help, it beats wallowing in self -pity!"

"Before we talk about the Major, I have a couple of other questions to ask, if that's okay?"

"Fire away."

"What can you tell me about Stanley Cross's daughter? Have you met her? I could do with some background."

"Stanley is one of the kindest men I've ever met, he is a proud, generous, and caring and good fun to boot. Well, he was, until his step-daughter turned up."

"Did you say step-daughter?"

"Yes, that's right, Stanley Cross is a quiet man, he was a factory supervisor at a men's shoe manufacturer, a confirmed bachelor. Then, the owner, Gerald Finch, died, and his widow, Sheila, took over the business and fell in love with Stanley. Sheila was a kind and funny lady, but her daughter, Sharon, is something else."

"What do you mean?"

"Vile woman, loud, lewd with a harsh tongue and greedy, so bloody gluttonous. Totally spoilt as a child and ruined, to cut a long story short, Stanley and Sheila married and lived a modest but happy life together for the next twenty years until Sheila developed breast cancer, it was discovered late and, most unfortunately, was invasive. It ripped through her body; Stanley nursed her throughout. He was heartbroken when she passed, he tells me not once did Sharon visit her mother when she was ill, even though she lived less than a mile away."

"That must have hurt. If you don't mind my asking, how was Stanley able to afford to live at Fairview? "

"Much to his utter surprise, Sheila was a wealthy woman, a few years after Gerald's death, she sold the factory and banked the assets. All of it went to Stanley in her will. Sharon was none too pleased, actually, that's an understatement, apparently, she caused quite a scene when told by the family solicitor. Of course, she took the matter to court, and lost, lost the appeal too. Then, about eighteen months ago, out of the blue, she appeared at Fairview and sold Stanley a sob story about being unemployed, said she was about to be evicted and his grandchildren, numbering four, were about to be made homeless."

"Don't tell me Stanley gave her money."

"Oh yes, the lovely man gave her fifty thousand pounds, but she soon returned with her sidekick partner Gary, for more. I begged Stanley to tell someone what was happening, but he said he could handle it, but you see he couldn't."

"Poor Stanley, just one more thing, I don't suppose you know if Sharon has a tattoo at all?"

"I do, couldn't miss it, it's an abomination on the left ankle."

"Are you able to describe it?"

"A crude outline of a hovering cherub," said Ada, pulling a face.

"Thank you, Ada, that's helpful, now, do you feel up to talking about the Major?" Harriet saw the minutest frown flit across the old lady's features.

"I'm going to have to face it sometime, might as well be now, but I need a glass of sherry first." Ada got to her feet and went to a cabinet where she removed a large glass; she picked up another and waved it at Harriet, who shook her head. Ada reached for a bottle on the side and poured herself a large measure, she took a large gulp as she walked back to her chair.

"That's better! Before we start, can I ask you a personal question?"

"Go ahead."

"Have you ever been truly in love, felt an almost overwhelming, engulfing emotion towards another which was reciprocated?"

"Gosh, I wasn't expecting that. It's complicated."

"No, it's not. It's a simple enough question."

"Well, yes, and no, by that I mean."

"Why do you look so sad?"

"Because I literally have just had the feelings, you describe a few months back and had them returned, but then the guy left to work abroad, and now, well, I just don't know if we will survive the separation."

"Where the devil has he gone?"

"He's a surgeon and, before we met, he volunteered for 'doctors without borders' or 'Médecins Sans Frontières." He's in Yemen."

"Oh, I see, but that's not insurmountable. I'll let you into a secret; I first met George Moore over forty years ago, a friend introduced us at a dinner party. He was such fun, open, well read, funny, and full of energy. I was not looking for love. No, it was the furthest thing from my mind, but he got under my skin. We met for coffee and then, as time went on, we would go to the theatre or a museum together. He was the personification of patience. Gradually, I melted and then boom!" Harriet couldn't help but chuckle.

"Can you believe it? I was in my late thirties and suddenly, for the first time, madly, passionately in love and my god Harriet, the sex was amazing; it was addictive. I was so happy, so elated all the time, and then George got posted to Northern Ireland. It hadn't occurred to me that this might happen we had just been living in the moment, it wouldn't have been so bad if we could have kept in touch, but he was part of a special unit and communication with the outside world forbidden. I didn't handle the situation well, went into a downward spiral, could barely hold it together at work. After six months with no contact, I decided I had to step away. I wrote him a letter explaining he was the love of my life, but that I just couldn't live like this. He'd abandoned us, or so I thought. I posted the letter to his unit HQ, and that was that. What I didn't know until years later was, he'd been involved in a horrific car crash late one night in which he received life changing injuries. They placed him in an induced coma for several months. By the time he recovered enough to look for me, I'd left my employment without leaving a forwarding address."

"Oh Ada, that's so sad." Harriet welled up.

"It was so stupid and so selfish of me, I still to this day don't know why I didn't try harder to find out where he was, what he was up to. It was so out of character, and when I think about it, I kick myself. I made it all about me, how I was feeling without even considering George, I basically brought years of yearning and sadness upon myself." Ada emptied the last of the sherry from her glass, as Harriet rose from her seat and put her arms around the fiercely proud and complex woman before her.

Wiping a tear from her eye, Harriet took Ada's hand. "Don't be so hard on yourself, I'm pretty sure in all our lives we are guilty of behaving in a way that years later we just can't fathom. Six months is an eternity without contact, the absence must have been extremely hard, but you reunited, how did that happen?"

Ada's face lit up for a second, "it was quite by chance, I had been living here at Fairview for about two weeks when one evening at dinner one table was being raucous, a birthday celebration I believe. Amidst the dining room noise, I heard a laugh boom out, once heard, George's laugh was never forgotten."

"What did you do?"

"For an instant I froze, then I got to my feet and looked around the room, on the far-side by the garden doors was a round table with eight diners. In the middle, in a wheelchair, sat George tucking into beef stew. He must have sensed me, for at that very moment he looked up and we locked eyes, never have I wanted to run away more. I was petrified he would reject me, send me packing, show me up in front of the other residents as the one who'd forsaken him, Lord knows, I deserved it."

"But?"

"But a massive grin spread across his face as he carefully placed his knife and fork on his plate and manoeuvred his wheelchair from under the table. He sped across the floor shouting, "I knew we would be reunited, my love!"

"At that point, I wept, I remember tentatively moving towards his open arms, when I was close enough, he grabbed me, and I flew into his lap. He hugged me so tight; I could hardly breathe and then he kissed me, and I was lost. And everyone in the room erupted into spontaneous clapping and cheering. A second chance had revealed itself, most of us are not lucky enough to get that. From that point on, we were pretty much inseparable, I was giddy with happiness. Rita, on the other hand, was less than enamoured by the relationship and lectured us one afternoon on what she considered to be the proper way to conduct ourselves. Which, of course, we ignored!"

"How wonderful you found each other again, what were the chances? It must have been fate."

"I agree, Fate. Now, don't you lose your man without at least putting up a fight."

"I won't, you've inspired me, Ada."

"Right, then, it's time to tell you about discovering George's body."

A couple of hours later, Ada had recounted that morning in extraordinary detail, as Harriet took copious notes.

"As I told Rita at the time, there was something very wrong about the situation and there was something missing, which I still can't put my finger on, I keep hoping it will come to me, it's so very troubling and annoying that I can't recall what it is."

"It's probably the stress of the situation, give it time, it may come back to you." Harriet glanced at the watch on her wrist, it had belonged to her father, and she found comfort in wearing it.

Ada jumped to her feet, "oh my God, what are the chances? Yes, of course, of course."

Harriet raised an eyebrow.

"I've remembered, it was his Rolex watch, the only time he ever took it off was to bathe and at night when he placed it in a small dish on his bedside table. Only, I remember now, it wasn't there that morning."

"Well, done Ada, I don't suppose you recall what type of Rolex it was do you?"

"I most certainly do, a rare a vintage 1974 Rolex Submariner with a single line of text, i.e., 'Submariner' in red above the six o'clock."

"Any idea of its worth?"

"At least twenty grand, if not a little more."

"Bloody hell, we might just have a line of enquiry to pursue here."

"I don't understand?"

"Well, it's suspicious, George, who is in good health, suddenly dies, and his expensive watch is missing. Based on what you've just told me, it seems likely the watch was taken, what we don't yet know is if it's linked to his death."

"Sorry, can you spell it out to me in layperson's terms?"

"Okay, the watch was probably stolen, so we can look at pawnbrokers, and ask around local jewellers, to see if anyone has recently tried to sell it and if they have, there will be records which might allow us to identify the person who brought it in. They will be of interest to us for the theft, but also if, it turns out George didn't die of natural causes."

"Okay, now I get it, good."

"Thank you for the detail you were able to provide Ada, it really is extremely helpful."

"You are most welcome dear, although I have to confess, I now feel completely knackered!" Harriet laughed, as she got up from her chair.

"I'm afraid I must go, I've got a meeting, but I'll be back tomorrow if that's okay, to cover more questions?"

"I look forward to it Detective Sergeant Lacey, now don't forget to contact your new man tonight."
"I won't, see you tomorrow."

Harriet started to walk towards the door before pausing, she turned around. "Ada, do me a favour, keep your wits about you, don't go talking too freely, keep a low profile until we've worked out what's going on here."

"Don't worry about me, I'll be the personification of discretion." Ada winked at the beautiful young detective before her.

Ethel Moore was a strange looking woman, she very much reminded Harriet of the character Nora Batty from 'the last of the summer wine,' a sit com, popular in 1980's. The character routinely wore thick stockings, plain dresses, a flowery overall and baggy cardigan, and big comfy flat shoes. The woman sitting across from her was dressed almost identically, Harriet guessed she was in her early to mid-sixties, but she looked older. Ethel was on her guard, arms clasped tightly across her bosom.

"Ethel, there's nothing to worry about, this is an informal chat, my name is Mike, and this is Harriet, we'd just like to ask you some questions, if that's okay?" Mike used his most diplomatic voice. Ethel said nothing.

"We understand that as part of your work, you provide the residents with their night-time cocoa? Ethel merely nodded.

"Okay, and this is every night?" another nod, "can you tell us what time your round starts and ends?"

"Why? Has someone been complaining? Cos they're a lot of over indulged whingers."

"Oh, I see. Well, no complaints; we are looking at some unexplained events and are asking all the staff some routine questions."

At this, Harriet noticed Ethel visibly relaxed the grip on her bosom. "So, when is your round each night?"

"Between 9.30 and 10pm, well, it's supposed to be, but I'd have to be bloody 'wonder woman' to get round everyone in that time. I rarely finish until 10.30pm."

"Ethel, does every resident take cocoa at night? "Asked Harriet.

"Most do, one or two don't, Ada Brown for one."

"Did you notice anything out of the ordinary at all the night Major Moore died?" Asked Harriet.

"Nope, same as always."

"Does the Major routinely take Cocoa?" Asked Mike.

"He does."

"And that night?" Asked Harriet.

"I don't recall, but then I can't remember when he's ever turned it down."

"Did you tend to anyone during that night?" Asked Mike.

"Nope."

"Just talk us through your routine, would you?"

"I fetch the trolley from the kitchen, I pour the cocoa from the thermos jugs, I give the spoilt brats their bedtime drink, I put the trolley back in the kitchen."

"You don't much like your job then," observed Mike.

"Jobs alright, it's the people."

"Well, thank you Ethel," said Mike.

"Just one last thing, are you by any chance related to Major Moore?"

Asked Harriet.

"Nope."

On the drive back to the office, Harriet could not contain herself, "Mike, is it me, or is Ethel about as unlikeable as they come?"

"She is, and as surly and disagreeable."

It was two o'clock in the morning, Ada knew this because she'd been clock watching for hours. It was no good; she had to go for a walk. It had been a week since she'd last ventured out in the middle of night and just for a moment, the desire to let out a 'whoop' of joy at the sense of freedom overcame her, for she so enjoyed her night-time adventures.

Thirty minutes later, she was savouring a cup of cocoa in Mr Aubert's chair in the old scullery, her feet in their usual position, on the log burner, when a hefty arm grabbed her around neck and a sweaty palm covered her mouth.

"You fucking meddling bitch," said a deep slurring voice in the darkness. "Don't think you're going to spoil what I have here," it hissed.

Unable to respond; Ada noted her female attacker was strong, built like a Russian shot putter.

"I'm not stupid. I know it was you who made the police suspicious, you silly rich bitch." Still, Ada could not reply; pinned to the chair, her mouth continued to be covered by a clammy palm. There would be no use trying to resist, for she now found herself gagged and blindfolded. Then her captor tied her hands behind her back with some type of rope, she was no match for this burly bully, next, they unceremoniously threw her over their well-padded shoulder and carried her out of the scullery and down a hallway. There was a left turn, then a right turn, then another left turn, a key in a lock, a door creaking open. Then the descent down some rickety steps, Ada could feel the rungs wobbling beneath them. The air became increasingly cold and smelt musty, Ada's kidnapper mumbled under her intoxicated breath, off the shoulder, her fall cushioned by a mattress. She remained blindfolded and tied, but at least her captor removed the gag.

"What's the matter? Cat got your tongue?" rasped her kidnapper, now very much out of breath, this time Ada chose not to reply.

"Suit yourself, now stay here while I decide what to do with you." Ada could hear her attacker lumber back up the steps, cussing as she went, the door closed, and a key turned in a lock, she was alone in the dark.

Ada pondered her situation, at least she was unharmed, and she was wearing her padded dressing gown, which afforded some protection from the cold, but no one knew where she was, and it was pitch black. There was no getting away from it, she was in deep trouble.

CHAPTER 8

Odell regained consciousness slowly, her head hurt; she put her hand to her temple and found a large tender lump. Slowly, she forced her eyes open, but everything was hazy. Aware of movement, to her left, adrenalin kicked in and her breathing became laboured, it took a terrifying moment or two to focus, for her vision was blurred. But to her utter relief, it was a grinning Maximus who came into view, he hastened to her side, cupping her head in his hands he gently kissed her face, she did not resist.

"Thank the gods you are alive; I was so scared you would not wake up and then what would I say to Ma?"

Odell laughed despite the pain, "please tell me what happened? I remember climbing onto the big man's shoulders and then it's a blank."

"You saved my life, the large man dropped me to the ground, you ran at him, jumped on his back, and kicked him forcibly in the ribs, in the process you fell and hit your head, but you bought me sufficient time to jump back up and thrust my sword into his side."

"Then what?"

"I ran across to you in a panic, you did not move; you were out cold. I picked you up in my arms and ran to the horses, the big man was thrashing about on the forest floor, blood spurting from his side, his cronies were also on the ground. You left them in various states of injury. I placed you across your horse and tied you to it, I then hastily picked up our belongings and lashed your horse to mine, we rode as fast as the horses would take us until night fell, then it was impossible to go any further. I found a small thicket and hid us for a few hours, as luck would have it, the moon was full and after an hour of rest or so, we set off again, it poured with rain, so I took the gamble there would be little or no traffic and we rode all day until we reached our first night's camp on the hillock, here."

"I am indebted to you," said Odell stroking Maximus's face.

"No, it is I who is indebted to you," Maximus moved in closer and kissed her on the lips, a tender kiss.

"Do you think they will come after us?"

"I think there's a very good chance they will try, with their injuries, I calculate it will take them a day or so to recover sufficiently to travel. Hopefully, by then, we will have disappeared without a trace, but just to make sure, we will travel at first light for a few hours and then hide. Now, it's important you eat, I've prepared some soup and then you must rest, for in the early hours we will once more set off."

Odell did not have the energy to argue, for the first time in many years, she was happy not to be in charge. The soup was flavoursome, she ate and then snuggled back beneath her blanket, it was then that maximus handed her a small bottle made of animal skin.

"Ma gave me this for emergencies," he said, handing it to her, she placed her lips on the spout to discover an aromatic sweet liquid filling her mouth, mead, she smiled and shared it with Maximus.

Odell shivered, "I'm sorry, it's not safe to keep the fire alight at night," Maximus tidied away. A few minutes later, with a blanket in hand, he laid down next to her. The warmth of his body was comforting, but it also triggered a fluttering sensation, a racing heartbeat. Maximus pressed his body against hers, as she lay in the quiet darkness, she was aware of his fragrance overwhelming her, she turned to face him, his lips met hers. Instinctively, Odell caressed his neck with her soft lips; she could not help herself, Maximus stroked her face and then her neck, for the first time in her life, Odell felt overwhelmed with longing. Each time Maximus touched her, she yearned for more until finally they came together in a hurried mutual hunger.

Before dawn broke, Maximus woke Odell with a kiss, they locked eyes for an instant before breaking camp and beginning the last part of their journey home. They rode carefully, down a steep grass slope that led away from the hillock and headed for the riverbank. Neither spoke of their night-time encounter, but as they rode, Odell mulled it over in her mind, smiling to herself as she did so. Her first experience of a man had been just about perfect, the old ladies of the settlement had often told stories of their first times, tales of disappointment, and occasionally violent and drunken liaisons. She had vowed never to take a man, but now, she just might reconsider.

They rode hard and fast and made good time, when they reached the far side of the hamlet of Blakeney, they turned away from the riverbank into Odell's beloved forest. The urge to keep riding was strong, but a dangerous option, so they found themselves a wooded hollow in which to rest until dusk. Within two hours of leaving the hollow, they approached the steep climb to the settlement, flushed with excitement, Odell led the way. As they neared the top of the trail, a shout rang out, Odell immediately recognised it as her brother Alwin, the vast settlement doors swung open to reveal a large crowd of eager, welcoming faces.

As Odell dismounted, Alwin flung his arms around her and held her tight.

"Whatever happened to you?" Screeched Ma, before approaching and hugging her granddaughter." Odell instinctively put her hand to her head.

"I fear we got into a serious fight," Maximus replied.

"I can see that, have you seen your face Maximus?" Asked Ma, with alarm, Maximus shook his head.

"Maximus saved my life," said Odell.

"Ditto," he replied, as Marcus strode across to greet them both.

Marcus threw his arms around Maximus and then Odell. Struck by how comforting she found his touch, Odell briefly nestled into his chest.

Three weeks later, everyone gathered once more at the settlement gates. All Odell could think of was her last conversation with Marcus and Maximus. It had started with Maximus telling her it was time to leave before the autumn storms struck; he told her he had no choice but to go; he needed to sort out his affairs, but he intended to ask his wife for a divorce, leaving him free to be with Odell. Odell had reflected that in her world, things were much more straightforward. Women were free to align themselves to men with no ceremonial tie. The news that Marcus was to accompany Maximus was almost too much to bear, he too swore to return, but this was cold comfort to Odell. She knew she was unlikely to set eyes on either man again.

An overwhelming feeling of misery threatened to engulf her. She had to fight to keep her composure; so much had happened since last winter when she'd come across the starving soldiers. From hatred and distrust had grown warmth, mutual respect, and friendship.

"It is with deep sorrow that I take my leave," said Maximus, "we can never fully thank you for all you have done for us, I am pleased that some of my men have chosen to stay and make their future here, I too intend to return as soon as I am able."

"May the gods look out for you all. My heart is here; I look forward to the day when we will once more be together." Marcus turned to wave to Odell. For the slightest moment, their eyes met, betraying his reluctance to leave, but it was his duty. He owed Maximus his life.

"Safe journey, my friends. Keep to the riverbank until you reach the settlement at the mouth of the estuary. Make for the port area where an old man wearing a burgundy cloak will meet you. Hand over your horses and he will take you to your vessel. May the gods be with you." Called out Ma. Odell was grateful to her grandmother for taking charge, for such was her sense of sorrow she felt unable to utter a single word.

As the weeks passed, Odell's mood darkened. She could not pull herself out of the gloom she felt and took to spending many hours in the forest alone.

Sometimes she hunted, often she brooded, it wasn't just that she was missing her new friends; it was deeper. She was so preoccupied by her thoughts that she began to take risks.

One evening she found herself in an area of the forest she'd not visited since she and her father had hunted deer there many moons before. Only when she realised the light was fading did she recognise how far from home she was, she ran much of the way back, surprised that she could still recall the route, but when she reached the settlement, she found a distressed Ma by the main gate.

"Did he find you? Please tell me he found you?" she screamed, tears rolling down her cheeks, her eyes searching beyond Odell for someone.

"Who? Did who find me?" asked Odell.

"Alwin."

"What do you mean, Alwin?"

"When you were late, he was worried sick and, despite my forbidding it, he ran off to find you."

Odell's cheeks drained of colour as she steadied herself against a nearby tree trunk, her mind racing.

"There's still some light left, we will have to work fast." Within minutes Odell had organised search parties and sent them off, one to the south, one to the north and one to the east with strict instructions to Julius, Freya's admirer, and the other soldiers to keep a low profile, to stick together and return before it became pitch black. Odell searched in the west and alone, she could not trust her emotions. Ma stayed behind with Freya to guard the settlement gate.

Instinctively, Odell went into hunter mode, in a matter of minutes, she'd picked up signs of activity, horse hooves in the mud, crushed bracken, she followed the muddy trail to the fishponds, but here it went cold. Just as she was wondering what to do next, she heard a cry on the breeze, and set off in that direction, she was helped by the sound of a second yelp. As she turned the corner, she could not help laughing, for there was Edgar, Alfred's second in command, rubbing his ankle.

"I might have known this bastard belonged to you," sneered Edgar.

"Nice to see you too, Edgar, now give me back my brother."

"Your brother's a man now and he's coming with us," Harriet could see Alwin's arms were tied, his eyes betrayed fear, one of Edgar's grunts held him by the shoulders.

"He's not, and he is not."

"I've had enough of your bravado, you snooty dalcop (dull head). Alfred's not here, so you can't rely on his good nature, I'm going to teach you a lesson."

"This should be interesting," Odell muttered under her breath.

"What did you say? You old hag." And with that, Edgar threw a punch, his men sniggered, as it missed its target, enraged by his loss of face, Edgar drew his knife from his belt and lunged towards Odell, who deftly kicked it from his hand.

"I've heard the rumours, I know you're shielding filthy roman scum, mark my words, I'm coming for you all."

"You speak utter rubbish, Edgar, your problem is that your bark is louder than your bite, I'm not in the least bit afraid of you."

A scowling Edgar ran full pelt at Odell and a sparring match began as they moved backwards and forwards, striking blow after blow at each other, Edgar became more and more red and breathless, yet refused to yield. The fighting continued until Odell kicked Edgar in the face, he fell to the ground, she dashed towards the man holding Alwin, he jumped out of her way, and she untied her brother.

"Run Alwin, run," Odell turned to face the group of bandits, arming her bow, but none showed any appetite to engage. So, she turned and ran into the undergrowth to freedom, it did not take her long to catch up with Alwin, they hugged in the darkness.

"I'm sorry sis, I was so worried about you, you've not been yourself lately, I thought I might lose you and I couldn't bear it. You were amazing back there by the way, you do know I miss Maximus and Marcus too?"

"Oh, Alwin, I didn't mean to cause you worry, and I know you do. You formed a deep friendship with Marcus, it must be hard now he's gone, I've been very selfish, wallowing in my personal misery without a thought for anyone else. Come on, my brave warrior, let's get you back to the settlement, and with that they ran through the moonlit forest.

"Do you think Marcus and Maximus will return as they promised?" asked Alwin as they ran.

"It's in the hands of the gods, but I hope very much that they will."

"Me too."

As they reached the ponds a wolf howled, then another, piercing the silence, they immediately picked up their pace.

Next morning Odell was nursing a severe beer induced headache. She smiled as she recalled how the whole settlement had come together to eat, drink, dance, and sing in celebration of the safe return of Alwin. And whilst she still missed Marcus and Maximus with the same intensity, she now saw she had a responsibility to the settlement, winter was coming, they must prepare if they were to survive.

Every so often she would visit the place where she'd first found the Roman soldiers, it helped her to feel close to them amongst the majestic pine trees and boulders. And besides, it gave her the opportunity to search through the belongings they'd left behind, for something useful, a knife, a tool, a coin or two. Rarely were her finds surprising, but one winter's day, she came across a rock formation at the back of the camp, as she approached, it looked almost man made. On closer inspection, she saw the glint of something in the middle of the stones, intrigued, she lay on her stomach and reached in, her fingertips found a hard form wrapped in cloth in its midst, adjusting her position so that her shoulder was tight against the stone, she stretched her arm in and, after several attempts, her fingertips grabbed hold of the cloth. She yanked and yanked again, whatever it was, it was stuck. Carefully, she moved some stones out of the way and tried again, and again, eventually, she wrenched the item out. Carefully she peeled away the layers of cloth to reveal a long old wooden pole or staff, towards the top of the pole was a tattered red and gold embroidered flag, *'Legio IX Hispana,'* and topping the pole, a bronze eagle. Odell gasped at its beauty, instinctively, she knew it was an important and valuable find, she would need help to recover it, but who could she trust? She placed it back in its hiding place until she could figure what to do.

CHAPTER 9

Present Day:

Lately, Harriet dreaded Friday evenings, tonight she returned home feeling wearier than usual, the last thing she wanted was a fight with Amelia. She threw her bag down in the living room and kicked off her shoes before putting the kettle on. With a steaming mug of tea in hand, she sat at the kitchen table and took out her notebook, she wanted to make sense of the last few weeks, there was a briefing first thing Monday morning, Derek Wynn would expect an update, and this was a complex case. She made notes as she went over the events in her mind. They had only just scratched the surface, they needed to make many more inquiries to have a chance of working out what had been going on at Fairview.

What did they know? Well, the Post-mortem of Vera Mortimer had revealed undigested cocoa as well as alarmingly high levels of Fentanyl in her stomach. How had this opiate drug come to be there? Was it self-inflicted, or had someone dosed her with it? Further forensic tests would hopefully clear this up.

Eileen Graham's son had reported concerns of assault on his mother by a member of staff, her dementia and erratic behaviour were a problem, but the bruising on her wrists was clearly visible, and in an unusually lucid moment, she'd animatedly told Stanley Cross she didn't want 'cocoa'. Fairview employed Ethel Moore to provide residents with their night-time cocoa and see to their needs during the night, when spoken to, she had been sullen and bad-tempered and did not like the residents very much, but enough to harm them? When asked, residents described Ethel as rude and brash. Scenes of crime had found a bite mark on Eileen's arm using ultraviolet photography, was there enough to arrest and interview Ethel and compare her bite with the mark on Eileen? The cold cup of cocoa Ada had liberated from the kitchen had tested positive for Fentanyl, there would need to be some inquiries into access to the kitchen in the evenings, and some profiling and background checks on all staff, they would need to establish who was on duty when each of these incidents occurred. It was then it dawned on Harriet if the results of the Major's post-mortem showed high levels of fentanyl too, it would suggest that more than one dose of fentanyl was being administered, one in the cocoa and one by some other means. There was also the matter of the Major's missing Rolex watch, this would need looking into, as well as inquiries into whether there were also items missing from Vera Mortimer's room.

Regarding the Whistle-blowers' calls to the Care Quality Commission, phone logs would need to be examined and those who'd received the calls spoken to. Harriet hoped that interviews with Fairview's staff might prompt the caller to come forward, it was also vital to find out if other deaths needed scrutinising, but over what period? The Families of residents would need to be contacted, did any of them have concerns over their loved one's passing?

Finally, at least for now, was Sharon Dean's assertion her step-father Stanley Cross was being assaulted by a member of staff. She had provided some poor CCTV footage; this had been sent off to be enhanced. Mike suspected Sharon had concocted the allegation as part of a plan to sue for compensation. It was time to see what the covert camera had captured, as well as what Stanley's bank records yielded. Ada was scathing about Sharon and accused her of extorting money from Stanley, she had also confirmed Sharon had a tattoo on her left ankle. There would need to be a comparison of this with the tattooed assailant shown on the footage provided by Sharon. Harriet had just put her pen down when her sixteen-year-old daughter Amelia appeared in the Kitchen dressed in the tiniest black leather skirt and plunging crop top, it was all Harriet could do not to react.

"Hi Mum, you, okay?"

"Yes, thanks love, but I'm so glad it's Friday evening, it's been a long week."

"Me too! Party night!" Said Amelia as she danced around the kitchen, her loose, curly, red, hair swung through the air like wings, as she twirled around.

"It looks like you have plans?" Said Harriet.

"Yep, I told you on Tuesday as I left for school, Gemma Atkins has a party tonight at her house, everyone's going and staying the night."

"Did you?"

"Don't start Mum, I told you, I'm getting picked up by Molly's dad in twenty minutes."

"Well, I don't recall that conversation, and, I don't recall saying you could go, I'll give Gemma's mum a quick call to confirm."

"Don't! You always do this; you don't trust me at all do you?" Amelia stamped her foot hard on the kitchen floor.

"It's not you that I don't trust you. I just need to make sure you are safe."

"This is so fucking unfair. You are only doing this to show me up."

"Look, I'm sure it will be fine, but I need to check. You know that."

"Why can't you be like my friend's parents? You are so fucking uptight, and so old-fashioned, and you're only doing this to spoil my fun. I don't remember you doing this when Ben was sixteen. "

"First, please watch your language. Second, I'm not trying to spoil your fun, and third, your brother Ben hardly ever went out, but when he did, I checked."

"I'm not a fucking child!" Amelia stormed off upstairs; that's exactly what you are, thought Harriet, searching her mobile for Gemma's mum's number.

Ten minutes later, Harriet found Amelia in her room, re-applying her lip gloss.

"So, I presume Gemma's mum put your mind at rest. How embarrassing. I bet you were the only parent to ring up."

"Well, I was the first to ring. Look, I'm sorry, but it's not good news. There is no party."

"What the fuck!"

"Amelia, stop swearing!"

"What do you mean? There's no party, no party for me, I suppose!" Amelia's eyes filled with tears as she threw herself on the bed and let out a theatrical wail.

"No party for anyone."

A wide-eyed Amelia immediately stopped crying and turned to face her mother.

"Gemma's parents had planned to stay with friends this weekend, leaving Gemma in the charge of her older brother. Gemma decided it presented the ideal opportunity to arrange a party."

"Oh my God!"

"Yes, indeed."

"What did Gemma's mum say exactly?" Amelia sat upright.

"She thanked me for calling and checking. She was quite emotional."

"What, angry?"

"No, sad, she told me she felt let down by Gemma and upset other parents hadn't made contact."

"That's it, I'm dead now when her mum tells her it was 'The Lacey's' who blew her in, I'm finished, I'll have no friends! And you did this to me. I hate you, I hate you, you've ruined my life."

"That's enough!"

Harriet closed Amelia's bedroom door and went downstairs. She could hear her daughter raging and shouting and tried to ignore it; she didn't need drama tonight. As she put some potatoes in the oven, she heard the front door slam. A quick search of the house confirmed Amelia had gone. Harriet tried her mobile, but she did not pick up. For an hour, she tried to make contact, but to no avail. Now she was concerned. Amelia was normally a level-headed, conscientious teenager, but recently she'd become quite hormonal and with that came mood swings and poor decision making. She was out in the dark on her own; she was angry and upset, and even though she felt invincible, Harriet knew there was a darker side to life that required respect.

Not sure what to do, she considered driving around the local neighbourhood, but perhaps Amelia would calm down and make contact. Two hours passed, and just at the point Harriet knew she had to do something, her mobile sounded.

"Harriet, it's Kate, I have Amelia with me, she's fine."

"Oh, thank goodness, thank you, Kate, I'm so relieved and so grateful."

"It's no problem, she came straight here, and we've had a long chat, she's quite emotional, so is it okay if she stays here tonight?"

"If you're sure, that's kind of you."

"You know how much I love your kids, it would be a pleasure, but before I put the phone down, Amelia would like to speak to you."

"Sorry Mum, sometimes I don't know why I'm such a bitch, I just can't seem to control my temper, I didn't mean to scare you," mumbled her daughter.

"I'm just glad you're safe, we can talk tomorrow, I love you, you know that don't you?"

"I love you, too," the line went dead. Five minutes later, Amelia sent Harriet six emoji hearts and Harriet sent her daughter six back.

Tonight, had been the night Harriet had intended to speak to Henry Squires, Kate's dad, but it was late now, and Henry would be asleep, she checked her mobile, no message from him, she felt disappointed, but blushed in the darkness as she realised it had been at least four days since she'd last messaged him. Ada Brown's advice came to mind. *"Don't lose your man without at least putting up a fight..."* She determined to try harder as her eyes grew heavy and she drifted off to sleep.

Next morning, Harriet was pottering in the kitchen with a mug of coffee in hand when the doorbell rang, it was Mike Taylor, casually dressed in jeans and a jumper.

"Mike What a lovely surprise, what brings you here?"

"It's Ada Brown."

"Is she okay? Please tell me she is."

"Well, that's just it, we don't know where she is, she's simply disappeared."

"What do you mean? How is that possible?"

"No one has seen her since her carer Linda helped her to bed last night, this morning her bed was empty. Rita Pritchard has overseen a full search of the house and grounds but, there's no sign of her, Derek asked me to pick you up, he will meet us at Fairview with the police search teams."

"I hope she's okay, it was only yesterday I asked her to be careful, to keep a low profile." Harriet hastily grabbed her coat and bag. On the journey to Fairview, she texted Kate to ask her to drop Amelia off at her grandmothers, Harriet's mother, Jane.

A methodical and thorough search began, it was late afternoon when Harriet and Mike took a walk, they needed some fresh air, as they wandered back, Mike made a detour to the left-hand side of the house, Harriet followed. He paused by an old coal hatch, hands on his hips. "If there's a coal hatch..."

"There has to be a cellar," said Harriet.

"Exactly! I know the teams have searched a cellar, but it was on the other side of the house, this is an older part of the building, I bet you anything it's got two."

"Let's find out."

Rita Pritchard immediately sent for Fairview's handyman and head gardener, Ted Smith.

"Ted, how many cellars does Fairview have?" asked Rita.

"Well, that would be one, or one in use."

"Does that mean there's an obsolete one in the older part of the building?" Asked Mike.

"It does."

"How do we gain access?" asked Harriet.

"There's a door not too far from the old scullery, the key should be on a hook on the wall next to it, there's no electricity down there mind, and the stairs are dangerous, rotten, they wobble like mad. I've not been down there for years, are you sure you want to?"
"I don't think we have a choice, if there's even a slim chance Ada is down there," said a solemn looking Derek Wynn.

"I suggest we speak to the search teams and work out the safest route, could we perhaps enter via the old coal hatch? Put an officer on a rope? That way, we can control their descent." Said Mike.

"That's an inspired idea, Mike, how about Lewis?" Said Derek.

"He'd be perfect, small, slim, but strong," commented Harriet.

Half an hour later, James Lewis entered the coal hatch into the darkness of the cellar, a harness and a series of ropes were attached to him. It was eerily quiet for several minutes before a message came over the radio.

"Lewis to Chief Superintendent Wynn, over."

"Go ahead."

"Ada is here, and alive, as far as I can tell. She's unharmed, just cold and hungry, Sir."

"That's the best news I've had all day. Well done, James. Any idea how we get her out? Over."

There was a pause before James Lewis came back on the radio.

"Ada is extremely cold and stiff and presently unable to stand, I think we should have paramedics check her over, I suggest we drop a stretcher and a paramedic down the coal hatch, we will need to devise a pulley system to bring her up via the stairs, that does not place too much weight on them. How about asking the fire service to assist with their specialist rescue team? Over."

"All noted, will do. In the meantime, we'll drop some blankets and something for Ada to eat to you. Dusk is fast approaching, and I'd like, if possible, to get Ada out before darkness falls."

Harriet left the others and returned to Rita Pritchard's office, she had just sat at Rita's desk when there was a loud knock on the door, followed by a pummelling on the glass, Harriet jumped to her feet as Ethel Moore hurled herself into the room. Red-faced and puffy, she stood before Harriet, wringing her hands with tears streaming down her round face.

"Ethel, whatever's the matter?" Asked Harriet gently.

"I never meant to harm her; I would never hurt her. She's in the old cellar."

"It's okay, we've found her."

"Please tell me she's okay?" Ethel paced up and down the small office, muttering to herself, tugging at her hair.

"First signs are good. Now, please take a seat and a deep breath, and in your own time, tell me what's been going on."

Ethel duly sat, "I just don't know what came over me," she sobbed, "I'm not a bad person, I know I'm not liked, and I know I've been mean to the residents, but...," Harriet handed Ethel a box of tissues, she could feel the sadness emanating from her. "I knew something was amiss, but I was complicit, turned a blind eye. I should have spoken out sooner. Fairview is all I have. I have no home, no family, no friends; things just got out of hand."

Harriet placed her hand on Ethels, "how about we have a chat after you've composed yourself? Splash your face with water and put the kettle on in your room and I will come. We can have a cup of tea and you can tell me everything that's been going on. How does that sound?"

Ethel squeezed Harriet's hand and slowly rose from her chair; as she got to the door, deputy manager Sharon Jones appeared. Harriet noticed the two women lock eyes before Ethel scurried off.

"Sorry to interrupt, but they've extracted Ada; she's fine, but is asking to speak to you; you'll find her in the entrance hall."

"Thanks, I'll make my way there now."

Ada was on a stretcher; Harriet could just see her face, but her body was encased in a foil blanket. She carefully picked her way through the emergency service personnel until she was by Ada's side, she looked frail and old, but her face lit up immediately she saw Harriet.

"Oh Ada, it's so lovely to see you, we've been so worried about you."

"It's good to see you, too, I'm still bloody starving!" Harriet couldn't help but laugh. "I need to tell you two things, first who my attacker was, and second about something I found weeks ago, before George's death." Harriet moved in closer as Ada was whispering.

"Your kidnapper has already confessed, I'm about to speak to her, as for the other matter, I'll come and see you tomorrow or the day after, just as soon as you've recovered, okay?"

"Go easy on her, she's a lonely, sad woman, and I think you need to see to the other matter now, I believe it is important, besides, it's been playing on my mind. At the bottom of my double wardrobe are many shoe boxes, look for the third one on the left-hand side, middle row, a white box, take it and get the contents analysed. I'll tell you how I came to have it tomorrow."

"Okay, don't worry, see you tomorrow." Harriet briefly stroked Ada's cheek as the paramedics carried her stretcher towards the waiting ambulance.

Somewhat bemused by the contents of the shoebox, a paper bag containing a syringe, and an empty vial, Harriet went in search of Paul Jones from Scenes of Crime. Realising that she had been far longer than she intended, she dropped it off and gave Paul a hasty explanation before heading to Ethel's room. She knocked on the door, there was no reply, she knocked again; she tried the door handle, the door opened inwards; the room was in darkness. Feeling for the light switch with her fingers, she found it on the left of the door frame, as the room lit up, Harriet let out an involuntary gasp, at the blood pooling around her feet.

CHAPTER 10

410 AD Gloucestershire

It had been a crushing storm, the like of which only Ma could recall, it had caught the settlement off guard, descended upon them out of the blue. A harsh icy wind enveloped the entire forest, trees and saplings were bent double, the gale tore through towering ancient turrets with such force many were upturned, branches ripped away, flung through the purple, grey squall. The settlement suffered damage to huts, outbuildings, and animal pens, but the gods had been kind to them, for there had been no human casualties.

Odell stood by the entrance to her hut, surveying the damage, an eerie silence prevailed; the air was heavy, frozen, saturated, feathery flakes fell like goose down. The settlement's younger children ran around excitedly, catching the icy flecks on their tongues, laughing as they went. Odell pulled her cloak around her bony frame, the chill gnawed at her, and then she heard Alwin's unmistakable whistle from the lookout point. She listened intently, not foes, but friends, Alwin appeared from around the corner, his face animated. He beckoned excitedly for her to follow, she reached the gate as it creaked open, the sound of footsteps on the frozen ground, clouds of icy breath visible on the slope below. The other settlers were gathering, a growing sense of excitement imbued the camp.

As the travellers reached the gate, Odell scanned the approaching faces and let out a cry, a wide grin spread across her face, Marcus beamed back. Odell looked past him, then back, their eyes locked, he shook his head. Odell took a deep breath and sighed before running across to him. He scooped her up in his arms and embraced her, Odell thought her heart would punch a hole in her chest.

"You came back, you came back!" she yelled, half laughing, half crying.

"I promised I would, it just took longer than planned." Marcus looked past Odell now, for he had spotted Ma making her way towards him, she was holding the hand of a small boy. Marcus met her halfway; Ma passed the toddler to Odell before flinging herself at Marcus.

"For a filthy Roman, you are a sight, I'm so happy you're back, are you staying this time?" shouted the old woman, laughing, tears rolling down her leathery cheeks.

"If you will have me and my fellow travellers? We've been hunting and have brought food with us." A cheer went up from the hungry throng.

"Of course, we have missed you, Gladiator!" Ma hugged him tightly. The little boy shyly peered around Odell's right leg whilst maintaining a vice-like grip on her.

"And who is this little fellow?" asked Marcus, gently squatting down.

"This is Tamm," said Odell gently, suddenly nervous.

"There's no mistaking whose son he is, Maximus lives on." A flash of sadness passed over Marcus's face before his customary smile reappeared. Odell reached out for his expansive hands, which he gladly gave.

It wasn't until later in the great hall in the warmth of the firepit Odell and Marcus spoke.

"It is so good to be back, I can see you've had a tough time, you are painfully thin."

"I'm fine don't fret, but I won't lie, it has been hard, food has been scarce, and the weather, unkind. But, enough of this, I want to hear all about your journey, and of these men you arrived with, can they be trusted?"

"I can vouch for all of them, they are good, brave men."

"How did you come to be journeying together?"

"It's a long story, but essentially, they are all men who served with us. We stumbled across Felix at the port just as we were about to board our ship, he was trying to get passage aboard a vessel bound for Gaul, he'd been with the soldiers sent by Maximus to the Roman fort at Caerleon."

"Sorry, what was the name of the fort again?"

"Caerleon."

"Ah yes, I remember Maximus telling me about it."

"Did he? Well, Felix and the other soldiers never made it back there, he was the sole survivor of an ambush, left for dead, he was taken in by a border farmer who tended to his wounds. In return, Felix laboured for him until the desire to return home became too strong, eventually, he made it back to our camp, but of course, we were gone, so he followed the river down to the port."

"And what of the other two?"

"Titus and Cassius were sent by an increasingly desperate Maximus to Corinium, but they also failed to return, and then you stumbled across us, and the rest is history."

"Yes, but what happened to them?

A wide grin spread across Marcus's face, "would you believe it, they got lost. After days of travel, they reached Corinium, they were starving and weak, but the fort was abandoned. It appears they were only a matter of hours too late, it was dusk, too dangerous to continue, so they rested, ate the food left behind, gathered supplies, and discarded weapons. They planned to set off the next morning in pursuit, but they awoke to thick fog, and as fate would have it, they set off in completely the wrong direction. It was two days before they discovered their mistake, by then, it was pointless to even try to chase after the garrison. Eventually, they made it back to Glevum and took a boat down the river and onto Gaul."

"So, you didn't meet up with them here then?"

"No, they were in Rome but headed to Naples when word reached them Maximus was gravely ill."

"I see, and what of Maximus?" Odell took a deep breath.

"When we left that day, so many seasons ago, my heart was heavy; I was caught between duty and honour and an overwhelming desire to stay." Odell squeezed Marcus's hand.

"To begin with, all was well. We crossed the water to Gaul and rode hard and

fast through Germania and onwards until we reached Rome. Then we rode across the country to Maximus's estate on the bay of Naples. A beautiful place overlooking the sea, fertile soil, where vines, vegetables, and fruits thrive and there is an abundance of prey to hunt. The journey took many days, but

Maximus was upbeat, he was set on asking his wife to release him from their marriage, confident he would return to you."

"But" said Odell, sensing Marcus's hesitation.

"But, far from giving her blessing, as Maximus had believed, Flavia refused to release him; they fought for many weeks; relations soured to the point they barely spoke a word to each other."

"And?"

"And then one day we were out in the fields overseeing the pruning of the grapevines, distracted, no doubt by his argument with Flavia, Maximus cut his hand, it wasn't a deep cut, but it refused to heal, soon Maximus had a fever, and before long he was in and out of delirium. Despite the best physicians, opium for pain relief and quality vinegar to clean the wound, Maximus became weaker and weaker, until one morning, he was gone."

Odell placed her hand on Marcus's arm, "I'm so sad you've lost your best friend, and I'm sad you had to be the one to tell me about his passing, but I'm glad you are here, I've never told you this before, but we need you, I need you." They sat in silence, holding hands for some time.

"In the days before he died, something troubled him deeply. Semi-conscious, he was not making much sense, I tried my best to understand," said Marcus, looking at the floor.

"Of what did he talk? "Odell moved in a little closer.

"He repeatedly asked me to recover the eagle, to set it free. He pleaded with me not to let it fall into the hands of the emperor. Unfortunately, I did not know what eagle he was referring to."

"Why did he not want the emperor to have it?" Asked Odell.

"Emperor Honorius is widely seen as a disaster. The public views him as weak and clueless."

Odell closed her eyes, trying to make sense of what Marcus had told her, and then it came to her.

"I think I know what Maximus was talking about," Marcus's left eyebrow arched, "I will show you tomorrow if you like?"

"I should like that very much. There is something else," he said, pulling a ring from his pocket. "This was Maximus's family signet ring, it was his sincere wish it should be yours, as a token of his love." Marcus choked back tears as he handed it to Odell, a gold ring with a carved orange stone at its centre, she inspected it.

"It's beautiful, is that a leaf at its centre?"
"Yes, the stone is a type of quartz, highly prized, it's been carved with a vine leaf to denote Maximus's vineyard."

"I will treasure it, when Tamm is old enough, he will wear it to honour his father, in the meantime, I will wear it around my neck just like your tooth."

"I think that would be a fitting tribute to Maximus."

"Now please tell me how Maximus's wife Flavia took his death?"

"With dignity, she loved him deeply, it must have been profoundly hurtful; he didn't feel the same way."

Odell blushed, "I feel bad Marcus, what happened, I ..."

"There's no need to explain."

The next morning Marcus and Odell set about preparing for their hunting trip, food in the settlement was scarce, they needed to restock after the storm. As they were about to set out Marcus touched Odell on the arm.

"Times are changing, roman soldiers are leaving not only your land but other parts of the world too and with their departure, there is increasing lawlessness, in parts of the world, outlaws operate with confidence, our journey back was not without incident. I just think from now on we need to be cautious."

"What sort of incidents? "Asked Odell, looking directly into Marcus's large brown eyes.

"A group of barbarians set upon us in Germania, they ambushed us, we fought hard and escaped with the loss of only a horse or two, but, in Gaul, as we were approaching the coast, a large group attacked us at dusk. Cassius was thrown from his mount and hit his head; he was out cold, we feared for him, he recovered, but has no memory of the event, Felix also suffered severe bruising and lacerations. We are used to fighting, trained to fight, but we were lucky to survive."

"Do you think danger lurks in our beloved forest?"

"I do."

"Then from now on we will take precautions, each time we enter the forest, we shall take a lookout with us."

"Good idea, now let's hunt some deer." Odell nodded.

The hunting expedition exceeded expectations, three deer, two boars, and several brace of wild duck. Odell sent the rest of the party back to the settlement in order that she and Marcus could make their way to the abandoned camp.

"You realise we have already broken our agreement to keep a lookout with us at all times?" Remarked Marcus.

"I do, but I do not want anyone else to see what I'm about to show you."

"Is it something I should be concerned about?" Marcus was frowning.

"No, well, at least I don't think so, I think it might be what Maximus was referring to. To be honest, I don't understand its significance but, I believe you will, you may already know of it."

"I am now most intrigued," said a grinning Marcus.

They left their horses tied to a couple of trees and made the last bit of the journey on foot, and, just as she had the first time, Odell crawled to the edge of the ridge to check the coast was clear. As expected, the old camp lay quietly overgrown below them. They scrambled down the steep slope to the bottom, Odell beckoned to Marcus as she made her way to a rocky outcrop at the far end of the camp, lying on her stomach she reached in through a gap in the stones, this time, it was easier to grab the cloth and pull the item into the open. Odell got to her knees as Maximus crouched down next to her, he observed as she unwrapped a package to reveal an old wooden staff, on which was mounted a red and gold embroidered flag, topping the pole, an exquisite bronze eagle. Marcus reached out to unfurl the flag, Odell watched as his eyes widened, he took a large intake of breath.

"Maximus, Maximus, what were you up to?"

"What does it say? I could not read it, is it important?" Asked Odell.

"Oh, it's important alright," said a breathless Marcus, "the writing tells us this was the standard of the most famous Roman legion ever to exist, well, in my humble opinion anyway, the Ninth Legion."

"What is a standard?"

"It's a banner, a pennant or emblem, carried to identify the legion."

"Can you tell me a bit about this legion so that I can understand why it matters so much?"

"The Legion came into existence many, many years ago, long before you and I were born, it was part of the Roman invasion of your country in AD 43, it became the most northerly stationed legion, battle-hardened, tough, and loyal to Caesar. In AD 117, however, it simply disappeared. Can you imagine? Five and a half thousand men, gone, vanished. The legion remains an enigma, revered by Roman soldiers across the ages and the empire. Many have tried and failed to explain what happened to them, and now, here today, we hold in our hands the very core of their identity."

"Oh, Marcus, it's sad, I'm imagining their loved ones never knowing their fate."

"Indeed, what I don't understand is where and how Maximus came to have possession of it?"

"What do you think his plan was?" asked Odell.

"Good question and one I cannot answer."

"What should we do with it?"

"Another good question, and again, I have no answer at present."

"How about we put it back, until we, you, can figure out what to do with it?" Marcus nodded as he wrapped the staff in the cloth, neither spoke on the journey back, both were lost in their thoughts.

A few days later, Marcus found Odell behind the cowshed, cutting wood.

"Odell, I'm going to ride to the port at the mouth of the river with Cassius and Felix. I've written a letter to Flavia; I will entrust it to a messenger. Let us see if she knows anything about Maximus and the Ninth Legion."

"Are you sure that's wise? First, you stand out somewhat. Second, isn't there a danger such an inquiry might make Flavia suspicious or worse?" Odell stood with her hands on her hips.

"First, I believe you are referring to my height and my skin colour?" Odell nodded, "second, I believe she is the only person who might know, and, going back to your first point, I no longer look like a Roman, I dress in your traditional wool trousers and tunic, and I wear my hair long on both my chin and my head."

"You do, but you still stand out."

"Are you worried about me?" I'll be careful, I promise, but I can't rest until I find answers. I feel a responsibility to Maximus and to the Ninth Legion."

"Go then, see you at dusk."

As luck would have it, Marcus and his companions met with no resistance and returned in good time.

They spent the next couple of months toiling on the land and gathering foods to preserve for the winter months. Odell showed Marcus which plants to gather, they ate some fresh; they dried others to supplement their winter diet. Nettle tips, hawthorn leaves, hedge garlic, wild garlic, and wild chervil were but a few of the many plants foraged from the forest and nearby meadows. They also gathered some for their medicinal qualities, such as ground elder, to treat gout and yarrow to staunch bleeding and treat fevers.

Marcus and Odell worked tirelessly side by side. Over time, their little community grew. Alwin moved into his own hut with Senna, a tall, beautiful girl from a nearby homestead. Her parents, Ria, and Bri, also moved into the settlement. Bri, a blacksmith, was an enormous asset; now they could make and mend tools, swords, and knives. Bri showed them how to extract iron found in stones from the ground, hot charcoal melted the iron which ran out of the stone or ore and once cooled, they could beat it into objects.

Cassius, Titus, and Felix also found female companions and built huts in which to live within the settlement stockade. And Julius and Freya started a family together. Before long, they had three children under five. Ma, however, was showing the ravages of time, determined as ever. She insisted on being fully involved in settlement life, but Odell had noticed a decline in her mobility and strength.

One sunny morning in late spring Odell was hard at work washing wool when Tamm now a stocky little boy ran around the corner closely followed by Marcus, he was attempting to outrun his pursuer, weaving in and out of the settlement huts, but he just wasn't quite fast enough. Marcus caught the little boy and held him above his head, much to Tamm's obvious delight, then he threw Tamm into the air and caught him again and again, to squeals of delight. Odell could not help but laugh at their antics, as she stood watching her son with the gentle mountain of a man, she was struck by an enormous wave of emotion, best likened to being slammed to the ground by a charging boar. She clutched her chest, as she stood there, she realised what she had once felt for Maximus did not compare to her feelings for Marcus. Maximus had been an infatuation, a crush, a desire. Marcus just made her heart palpitate; she could not imagine life without him. He was the kindest, most compassionate, and selfless man she'd ever known; all his actions were for the service of others.

Odell took an intake of breath and walked towards him, her knees suddenly weak. Tamm, back on the ground, was drawing pictures in the mud, Odell stood on tiptoe and placed her hands gently either side of Marcus's face, she drew him down to her and kissed him fervidly. A huge grin appeared on his face.

"What?" she said, also smiling, neither broke eye contact, but they leaned in towards each other. Odell made a promise to herself that day, never would she leave this man's side.

One icy winter morning, Odell returned to her hut with an armful of firewood, to find Ma had fallen out of bed and was unconscious. Uncharacteristically, she stood rooted to the spot, but only for a second or two, such was the sense of dread that gripped her. She rushed over to her grandmother, caressing the old lady's icy cold cheek. Scooping her up in her arms, she placed her back in her bed and, with more firmness than she'd intended, sent Tamm to fetch Marcus. When Marcus arrived, he found Odell standing over Ma.

"Her breathing is laboured, her skin sallow, look at the large dark circles under her eyes, I don't think she's long for this world." Marcus placed an arm around Odell.

Ma remained unconscious for almost twenty-four hours, when she did awake, a weak finger beckoned Marcus across to her, he knelt at her side and put his ear to her mouth.

"Promise me, Roman, you will take care of my family," she whispered hoarsely.

"I promise Ma."

"You are a good man, a man of principle with a large heart. I have grown extremely fond of you."

"And I have grown extremely fond of you too Ma." Marcus had tears in his eyes.

"Odell?"

"I'm here Ma, I'm here."

"Promise me you will take good care of the Roman, he's family now."

"I promise Ma."

"Good, I wish to nap now," and Ma closed her eyes for the last time.

CHAPTER 11

Present Day:

For a split second, Harriet could not move, she was rooted to the spot, watching the deep crimson, sticky blood creep around her boots. Then her training kicked in and she ran across to Ethel, who was lying on her back unconscious, her face a bloodied mess. A deep cut ran from her left eye across the bridge of her nose to her mouth, Harriet felt nauseous, but checked and found the faintest pulse, she pulled her mobile from her pocket and dialled Derek Wynn.

"Sir, I need a paramedic in Ethel's room immediately, I also need Scenes of Crime and Mike."

"What in the world has happened?"

"Someone has attacked Ethel, I must go, I need to stem the blood flow, her pulse is weak."

"No problem, there's still an ambulance crew here, I'll send everyone to you now."

The ambulance crew worked tirelessly for an hour and a half to stabilise Ethel before rushing her to the hospital. Derek Wynn, at Harriet's request, made sure an officer accompanied her and stayed with her at the hospital.

As scenes of crime led by Paul Jones gathered evidence, Harriet, Mike, and Derek Wynn went to Rita Pritchard's empty office to discuss the situation.

"The scene has all the hallmarks of a frenzied attack, Paul Jones thinks a struggle ended with the attacker using a brass doorstop to smash Ethel's face in," said Derek Wynn, to no one in particular.

"It's fucking horrifying, that's what it is," said Mike, Derek nodded in agreement.

"I think the attacker may have been intent on making sure Ethel didn't speak to me," said Harriet.

"What do you mean?" asked Derek Wynn.

"Well, I'm just thinking it through but, Ethel came to see me this afternoon, she was upset, in tears, she kept wringing her hands. She told me it was she who put Ada in the cellar, but she had not meant to harm her, she was a broken woman, as she was speaking, I felt there was something she wasn't telling me."

"What exactly did she say?" Asked Derek.

"That she knew something was amiss, that she was complicit in it but had turned a blind eye, even though she knew she should have spoken out. Things she said had got out of hand, it was at this point I suggested we have a chat in her room, I thought she might feel more comfortable there, she went to splash her face with water and to put the kettle on. But I was far longer than I intended, just as Ethel was leaving Rita's office, Sharon Jones appeared and asked me to go to Ada. By the time I had spoken to Ada and spoken to Paul Jones, I'll explain about that in a minute, I'd been gone, I suppose, half an hour. More than enough time for someone to silence Ethel.

"It makes perfect sense, silence Ethel, before she can spill the beans," said Mike, running his right hand through his hair.

"I'm positive that I told no one where I was going, what I was doing, I spoke to Ada in a crowded entrance hall, yes, but neither of us mentioned Ethel by name." Harriet helped herself to a coffee.

"What were you going to tell us about Paul Jones?" Asked Derek Wynn. "Ah yes, well, when I went to see Ada, she asked me to retrieve something she felt might be important to the case, she said it had been playing on her mind. She sent me to her room with instructions to open her double wardrobe and retrieve a shoebox, she asked for the contents to be analysed and said she would explain tomorrow. The box contained a paper bag with a used syringe and vial, I took it directly to Paul Jones, gave him a hasty explanation, and headed to Ethel's room. "

"Just as I think we are making progress in this case, there's another twist, it's late now, I suggest we go home and re-convene tomorrow for a full briefing at 0830 hrs. I am minded to bring in more officers, we need to get on top of this, and there are just too many loose ends and too much work to cover." Said a frowning Derek Wynn.

Next morning the incident room at police HQ was buzzing with anticipation, it took Derek Wynn some time to bring everyone up to speed with events, he then moved on to specifics.

"Okay, let's start with Vera Mortimer, her post-mortem revealed undigested cocoa and high levels of fentanyl in her stomach. Paul and Steven, any results you can share with us from further forensic tests?"

Steven Leach jumped to his feet, a file in his hand, "yes, we now believe that there were two types of fentanyl in Vera's system, the first was administered via her cocoa drink, the second, and the fatal dose, injected between the big toe on her right foot." At this the room erupted into noisy chaos. Harriet turned to Mike Taylor.

"Bloody hell, Mike, that means we have a murderer on our hands? Doesn't it?"

"I'd say so, it is unthinkable that Vera injected herself, isn't it?" Harriet nodded vigorously.

After Derek Wynn had restored calm, Steven Leach continued, "I agree, this is a shocker, what we also know is the fentanyl in the Cocoa was in tablet form, we found remains of it in Vera's stomach. And, we also have the cocoa that Ada Brown liberated from the kitchen, which also tested positive for fentanyl, in ground tablet form. We are working on the assumption that there may have been two separate occasions where the drug was administered, and this may have involved two separate individuals, the question is, were they working independently or together?"

"Good work, anything else concerning Vera?" Asked Derek.

"Not from me," said, Steven.

"I have something," said Harriet, looking at Derek.

"Please go ahead."

"DC Lynn Davies has been making inquiries with staff and Vera's family, and a diamond brooch is missing from her belongings. They describe it as a large silver flower with six petals. On each petal, a carat diamond, in the middle of the flower, a three-carat diamond. We believe it is worth about twenty thousand pounds, it seems Vera wore it almost daily. Inquiries are ongoing with local jewellers and cash converters to see if we can trace it."

"So, it seems theft may be the driver of all this," said Derek.

"Potentially, we don't yet know if there are other thefts, although Major George Moore's Rolex is missing; we also don't yet know if the thief is involved in dosing the residents." Said Harriet.

"Good point, Paul. Are we any further forward with the forensics concerning Major Moore?"

"Not yet Sir, I'm hopeful we will get preliminary results back from the post-mortem in the next couple of days."

"Okay, thanks, let's move on to Eileen Graham. Unfortunately, her dementia means we struggle to communicate with her. We know she has bruising on her wrists, and that she seems to be fearful of Ethel Moore, whose job it is to provide residents with their night-time cocoa. Ethel also has another responsibility, to be available to residents throughout the night should they need anything. We also know that Scenes of Crime found a bite mark on Eileen's arm using ultraviolet photography, but are we any further along with our inquiries into this?"

"Sir, Harriet, and I have spoken to many of the residents who all describe Ethel as rude and brash. We also spoke to Ethel herself. To say she was unhelpful is an understatement, she's not an amiable woman. We'd had initial discussions about whether there was enough to arrest and interview her so we could compare her bite with the mark on Eileen's arm, but we could not progress this further, for obvious reasons," said Mike.

"Indeed, I will talk later about the complications that have arisen concerning Ethel. Onto Sharon Dean then, and her claim that Stepfather Stanley Cross is being assaulted by a member of staff. I know you think this is a scam, Mike, but are we any closer to proving this?"

"Yes Sir, I think we are thanks to some sterling work by Kate and Steven; I'll leave it to them to explain."

Kate Squires got to her feet, "Steven and I have studied the CCTV footage given to us by Sharon, it shows the rear of a female in uniform, she is leaning over Stanley and shaking his arm, it also shows the same female wagging a finger at him. What is interesting, however, is the trousers the female is wearing are too short and reveal a tattoo on the left ankle, consisting of a cartoon airborne cherub. We have just finished reviewing the footage from the covert camera, it has captured a female we know to be Sharon Dean assaulting Stanley on four occasions over a two-week period, the assaults take the form of kicking his legs and slapping his head, what is also clearly on show on each occasion is the tattoo of a cartoon airborne cherub on her left ankle."

"That's right," said Steven getting to his feet, "but there is more, having looked at Stanley's bank statements, we can see regular payments to Sharon

Dean of enormous sums totalling over £500,000." A gasp reverberated around the room, "as luck would have it, we can show that each payment corresponds to a visit by Sharon to Stanley."

"This is brilliant work team, Mike, I want you to work with Kate and Steven to put together a package for the arrest of Sharon Dean. Poor Stanley, how awful to have suffered in silence for so long, I presume this means he will have to leave Fairview with no funds, how can he stay?"

"As it happens, an anonymous benefactor whom I suspect is Ada, has saved the day, Stanley is to live at Fairview for the rest of his days," said a smiling Harriet. This was greeted with spontaneous clapping.

"Now, I'd like to welcome an old friend back to the team, Detective Sergeant Geoff Harvey. "An open-mouthed Harriet jumped to her feet and looked to the back of the room, Geoff looked well, he beamed at her.

"As many of you know, Geoff worked with us on our last case and when things sped up in this case, I reached out to him, Geoff is running a team to investigate, amongst other things, the calls to the Care Quality Commission. Do you have anything to report?"

"It's good to be here Sir, yes, I've spoken to the staff at the CQC who received the calls, and as a result, I'm confident it was the same individual. Phone logs show they made the calls at approximately the same time, 1700hrs on

Wednesdays, two weeks apart. The caller was female, she came across as young, and frightened. We are currently talking to all of Fairview's female staff in the hope this prompts the whistle-blower to come forward." Said Geoff.

"Good work, let me know if you make any breakthroughs. Now, what about the other piece of work?"

"We have contacted the families of residents who died at Fairview, with the help of Rita Pritchard, we've identified eight families who reported concerns about their loved ones' deaths. Interestingly, all these deaths occurred within the last twelve months, all were thought to be from natural causes."

"That's a surprising timeline, I imagined this may go back years, any ideas?"

"We're exploring the possibility the individual responsible may be relatively new to the staff team."

"Because?"

"Because these deaths took place in the last twelve months, so we are looking at members of staff employed within the last year or so to see if there is anything suspicious."

"Understood, thank you, Geoff."

"Okay, let's move on, there have been some further developments in the last twelve hours, which some of you will be unaware of. First, Ada Brown was kidnapped and subsequently rescued. Whilst she's relatively unscathed, she was tied up in a cellar at Fairview and Ethel Moore, who is the prime suspect for her kidnap, has herself become the victim of a vicious assault, she is currently poorly in the hospital." Derek allowed everyone in the room to comment to one another before he continued. "DS Lacey, I'd like you and your team to interview Ada tomorrow morning at the hospital, and then Ethel, if that is indeed possible. We need to discover exactly what has been going on before there is another suspicious death."

"Yes, of course, Sir."

"Finally, Paul, can you expedite the analysis of the used syringe and empty vial DS Lacey found in Ada's wardrobe?"

"Yes, Gov, already on it."

"Good, well before you all leave, I need you to pick up your new actions from the action allocator, good luck and we'll have another briefing at 1600 hrs tomorrow. Thank you all for your hard work."

As soon as the briefing had concluded, Harriet made her way across to Geoff Harvey and hugged him.

"Geoff, I can't tell you how lovely it is to have you on board, how are you? How's Helen?"

"Great to see you too, Harriet. I'm great, thanks and Helen is doing well, she's back tutoring."

"I'm so happy to hear that, you don't think by any chance she'd have room for Amelia?"

"Oh, I'm sure she would, by the look on your face, Amelia is causing you stress, and I remember her as such a sweet young girl!" Harriet rolled her eyes.

"You could say that! She's bright, but she's overconfident and hormonal, believe me, that's not a good combination!"

Geoff chuckled, "I'm sure Helen has dealt with far worse, don't worry, I'll get her to contact Amelia. All you have to do is pay for it!"

"Thank you, Geoff, that's an enormous weight off my mind."

The next morning, Harriet arrived at the hospital before nine, she shuddered as she entered the building, wondering if she would ever get over her antipathy for such places unfortunately, she often had to visit hospitals for work. It took a while to find Ada, who was not in her bed, not even on her ward but in a side room in the intensive care unit.

As Harriet entered, she paused for a second to view the scene before her, Ada, willowy and small framed, donned in an oversize hospital gown, seated in a chair next to a hospital bed containing a large heavily bandaged Ethel. A sizable hand engulfed the smaller one, the two women were chatting away, or rather Ada, was doing all the talking and, although Ethel's head was bandaged, it was possible to hear the odd giggle escape.

"Morning ladies," said Harriet, interrupting.

"Oh, good morning, Harriet, how lovely to see you," said a beaming Ada.

"And how are you both?"

"I'm fine this morning, thank you, but, as you can see, Ethel is worse for wear, but bearing up, isn't that right Ethel?" there was nodding from the bandaged Ethel. Harriet noticed, however, her hand grip Ada's a little tighter.

"Look Harriet, I know you're a police officer and all that, but I wondered if you would be so kind as not to prosecute Ethel for my incarceration. Her actions were of a lady who'd lost her way, a desperate act, and she's extremely sorry, isn't that right, Ethel?" Once more the bandages nodded, this time a little more vigorously. We all make mistakes in life; God knows I have! And I, for one, utterly accept Ethel's heartfelt apology. In short, I do not want to pursue a prosecution, is that clear?"

"Perfectly," Harriet could not conceal a grin, "I will, of course, need to discuss this with the boss, Derek Wynn, but I'm sure we can sort something out."

"Excellent, you see Ethel, I told you Harriet was amazing."

"Ada, I wonder if I might have a chat with you in private?"

"Yes, dear, but the lovely policeman outside the door will need to come in and sit with Ethel."

Something made Harriet look at Ada's eyes as she said this, although her voice was calm, her eyes betrayed concern.

"Of, course."

Harriet took Ada to the canteen for a cup of coffee and a scone.

"Ada, what exactly is going on?"

"Well dear, early this morning I visited Ethel to sort out our differences and to find out how she came to be so hideously injured, and by whom. We had just finished talking about my kidnap and Ethel was telling me how much she regretted her actions, how lonely she felt, how angry she was with life and how she'd taken that out on the residents, when we were interrupted by a visitor from Fairview."

"Who?"

"Sharon Jones."

"How thoughtful of her."

"Not exactly, as soon as she entered the room, Ethel squeezed my hand with such vigour, I almost cried out, her hands shook so badly, I was forced to put both mine on top of hers and pin them to the bed. I realised at that moment she was afraid of Sharon."

"So, what did you do?"

"Well, Sharon walked straight up to Ethel and asked how she was. Before Ethel could reply, I jumped in and told Sharon such were the nature of Ethel's injuries; the doctors were pessimistic she would ever speak again. Let me tell you, the look of relief on Sharon's face was palpable."

"Goodness me, what exactly are you suggesting, Ada?"

"Well, Sharon came to see how much Ethel remembered and whether she was still a threat."

"And you say this on what basis?"

"I like to think I am an excellent judge of character; until now, I have always liked Sharon. She is intelligent, extremely competent at her job, and treats the residents with total respect. But even I get things wrong occasionally. Have you ever noticed how impeccably dressed she is? Head to foot designer gear and she drives an expensive car, an Aston Martin. Unless Mr Jones is extremely rich, she can't afford her lifestyle, and I know from Ethel, Mr Jones is a school caretaker."

"Perhaps she benefitted from a large inheritance or a lottery win?"

"Perhaps," Ada raised an eyebrow.

"Okay, we can absolutely investigate Sharon's background, but what is the relationship between Ethel and Sharon? Why is Ethel so afraid of her?"

"That I cannot answer, but something has happened between them. I'm sure Ethel will tell all in due course."

"Once again, you amaze me, Ada; are you sure you've not had some sort of legal training? You're a natural detective."

"Let's just say I've had my share of exposure to the law. Many, many years ago, I was in a violent and destructive marriage. I survived, but barely; my husband was a police inspector protected by the police organisation. Time and time again, I had my complaints ignored. I'm not proud of the person I became for a while, but it was literally a case of fight for survival or die."

CHAPTER 12

410 AD Gloucestershire:

It was with a heavy heart Odell got dressed that morning, for it was time to say goodbye to her beloved grandmother, Ma. The woman who had nurtured her when her mother was no longer around, who'd guided her and given her the confidence to lead the settlement.

At dusk, everyone gathered. They had wrapped Ma's body in a woollen shroud fastened with her mother's treasured brooch. Alwin, Marcus, Julius, and Felix gently lifted and placed Ma onto a small cart decorated with bluebells from the forest. The cart moved off slowly, pulled by Odell's father's faithful and now elderly horse. Tamm and Alwin walked hand in hand at the head of the procession, the rest of the settlers lined up behind, carrying posies of spring flowers. The cart made its way to the far west of the hamlet to the highest point overlooking the forest. On a flat rocky outcrop, they had built a pyre.

Odell stood by her grandmother, flame in hand, head bowed, a deep sense of sadness washed over her. Tradition dictated she say a few words, but none came to mind, just a feeling of utter numbness, Marcus squeezed her hand, their eyes met.

"We stand together this day to celebrate the life and pay tribute to an extraordinary woman known to all of us as Ma, we remember her as a force of strength in bad times, and a joy in good. She was wise, brave, strong-willed, and proud. We come together to honour her and commemorate her life. Let us not weep, for if she were here with us now, she would chastise us and implore us to make merry in her memory. Ma, we will not forget you, your granddaughter Odell will continue to guide us and care for us, just as you did. Go forth into your next life in peace and we will rejoice in the memories you have left us." Marcus bowed his head in respect, before Marcus, helping Odell to light the pyre. A tremendous cheer went up, drums, flutes, and horns sounded, and the settlement came together in one voice to sing their farewell to a remarkable woman.

Odell stood to one side for a moment, her heart full of gratitude to Marcus for speaking when she could not, he had hit completely the right note. As she wiped away her eyes, she realised he was right, this was a time to celebrate a life well-lived.

That evening, everyone gathered in the long hut to feast on deer, wild

boar, wild duck, flatbreads, honey, nuts, and drink beer. They told stories and

danced and gave Ma a superb send-off. It was the end of an era.

One evening three weeks later, one of two hunting parties failed to

return to the settlement by dusk. Felix, Bri, and Marcus were missing, only

Alwin, Julius, and Cassius had returned safely.

Odell immediately put together a search party, with a deep sense of

foreboding in the pit of her stomach. Darkness hampered the search and

driving rain, soaked them, despondent, they reluctantly returned to the

settlement. As dawn broke, Odell, Julius and Cassius set out with Alwin's best

friend Atto, acting as a lookout, they left Alwin and Titus behind to guard the

Settlement.

The search party set out on foot and headed toward the Ponds, where

they knew Bri had been keen to look for wild duck, Odell searched the area for

signs they'd been there, as they approached the second pond, she spotted

muddy footprints and scuffs, broken foliage, and blood mixed with mud. Signs

of a struggle, Odell saw fear etched across Atto's face, she walked over to him

and placed her arm protectively on his shoulder.

They tracked deeper into the forest, after several hours, they stopped to

rest by a stream. They ate flatbread and curd cheese, no one spoke, all were absorbed in their own thoughts. After half an hour, Atto got to his feet to scout ahead, he had been gone less than a minute when he ran back, eyes and mouth wide open. This coincided with a blood-curdling scream in the distance. Out of breath, there was a nerve-wracking pause before he could tell what he'd seen.

"Vagabonds! A large, well-armed gang is just ahead, they have prisoners and are brutalizing one this very minute, I'm not sure, but I think it might be your cousin Alfred's second-in-command, Edgar."

"Did you see Felix, Bri, or Marcus?" asked Odell.

"I didn't hang around; I saw an enclosure of sorts where men appeared to be restrained."

"Okay, I suggest we loop around in a big circle so that we are on the far side of the enclosure, we should get a better view from there, if my memory serves me right, there is a small dell there which will provide cover."

After an hour, they found themselves by the cluster of trees Odell had remembered. They peered between the trunks and could see a camp of sorts, just in front of them, the enclosure Atto had seen. Odell searched the faces of the imprisoned men, but could not see Marcus amongst them, Edgar was clearly visible, hanging upside down from a tree, screaming like a stuck pig. As much as Odell disliked him, she did not like to see such barbaric abuse, a group of four loud and dirty-looking men were taking it in turns to beat him with a large stick.

Instinctively, she reached for her bow and placed an arrow across the shaft, adeptly, she shot two of the men, Cassius saw to the other two, their screams, brought others running from the four corners of the camp. Atto and Julius crawled to the edge of the enclosure on their stomachs, once there, they broke it open and set the imprisoned men free. They found Bri and Felix unharmed, but there was no sign of Marcus, Odell joined them a short time later.

"Good to see you both, is Marcus alive?" asked a flushed Odell. She wanted to know, but also feared the news might break her heart.

"And you, he is, but he's in a precarious situation, he's over there," Felix pointed to a large tree to the left of the camp. Tied to its trunk a bloodied-looking Marcus, "they have hurt him badly."

"I will kill them all, tear them limb from limb for this!" Spat Odell, her face reddening.

"And I will help you cousin," said a voice behind her, a voice Odell recognised only too well, Alfred. "We have been tracking these vagabonds for days, murdering thieving bastards, they have sacked several of our villages and raped our women, they need to die horrible deaths."

There was no time to plan, for a group of foul-smelling, baying men surrounded them, Alfred and his men and Odell and her group formed a circle and readied themselves for the assault to come. Bloody and violent hand to hand combat, limbs hacked from bodies, sometimes heads from torsos. A tall, muscular, unkempt man lunged at Odell with a small sword, she ducked and swung around, plunging a dagger into the man's side. He roared in anger and pain and ran at her, but again she avoided him by swerving sideways. He did not give up and ran at her again, this time, Odell stumbled and fell to her knees, as she looked up, his sword blade bore down on her. Just as the blade was within a hair's breadth of her face, something hit her attacker with force, knocking him completely off course. As Odell got to her feet, she realised Cassius had collided with the man, taking his legs from underneath him. Odell mouthed a thank you to her saviour. They were losing ground, but then reinforcements arrived, the men who'd been imprisoned in the enclosure. Although many initially ran off, most quickly returned to fight with Alfred and Odell. Finally, Odell was able to cut Edgar down, he collapsed onto the bloodied battlefield, she helped him to his feet, slowly, with pain etched across his features, he dusted himself off, his face, dirty and swollen. She waited for one of his inevitable insufferable comments, but it did not come.

"Thank you, I owe you my life, and the gods know I don't deserve the mercy you've shown me." Odell nodded to Edgar before running over to Marcus. As she reached him, he seemed to be unconscious, with the help of Atto and Felix, she cut him down, and propped him up against a tree, stroking his face, she kissed his mouth over and over. As she took a breath, an enormous smile appeared on his face.

"Odell."

"Marcus," Odell wrapped her arms around him, weeping openly.

"I thought I'd lost you; I thought my life was over." She cried.

"I'm still here, I'll always be here for you."

"You really do care for this Roman," said Edgar, limping across.

"With all my heart, I will never leave his side, so, if you're going to kill him, you'd better kill me too."

"I'd say he is the bravest man I've ever encountered, he refused to break, no matter what they did to him, not once did he cry out, not once did he show weakness. I'd say he's earnt the right to live out his days with you." Said Edgar, walking off, dragging his left leg behind him.

"Well, I never thought I'd hear such words from Edgar's mouth about a Roman," said an approaching Alfred.

"He's clearly bumped his head!" Jested Odell. Alfred walked across to Marcus.

"I hear from my men that you fought off five or six of these pigs with your bare hands, I also heard tell how you snapped their necks and when others overwhelmed you, you continued to fight, using your head to butt, your feet to kick, and your teeth to tear flesh. But, not only that, you also did your best to protect others to ensure you took the blame for their insurrection, I salute you, Marcus Atilius." Alfred punched his chest in tribute. Marcus pulled himself to his feet, agony etched across his face, slowly, he bowed toward Alfred in thanks.

Whilst Atto and Cassius were seeing to Marcus's wounds as best, they could, Alfred took Odell to one side.

"Cousin, I have always had the utmost respect for you, you are a free spirit, brave, feisty, untamed. I can see in your eyes how much this man means to you. Look after each other, we are entering a new post-Roman world and I believe it will become a darker and more violent place before we restore order. Be careful and take good care of your people, and I hope from time to time, our paths will cross."

"Thank you, Alfred, thank you for fighting alongside us and for your kind words. Marcus means the world to me; it is my one genuine wish to live out my days with him. What will you do now?"

"You know me, I must always have a crusade, a campaign. For the time being, it will be to rid the forest of these filthy, rotten thieves."

"Good luck with that! But I, for one, am glad."

"Here, take my horse, there's no way Marcus will make it back on foot. I'll send Edgar in due course to retrieve it, but don't go shooting him!"

"The Horse?" said Odell, grinning.

"No, Edgar! For all his faults, he is fiercely loyal to me."

"Thank you, Alfred, you are a good man."

It took several months for Marcus to recover from his injuries. At his insistence, the settlement relied less on hunting and more on agriculture. Bri fashioned ploughs and other farming implements, and they worked the land and kept a greater variety of animals to supplement their diet. Before long, they were growing enough wheat and barley to sustain them through the long winter months. They also grew peas, flax, and beans and increased their stocks of sheep, cattle, pigs, geese, and chickens.

As the forest trees turned a variety of yellows and oranges, Marcus took an active part in settlement life once more. One morning, as he was returning from the fields, Alwin stopped him in his tracks.

"Marcus, you have a visitor."

Marcus put his tools down and walked across. Alwin stepped aside to allow him to view the man through a small window in the gate. Marcus immediately recognised him as the messenger he'd sent to Flavia many months before.

Later the same evening, in the firelight of their hut, Marcus unrolled a scroll. "Odell, I have a reply from Flavia."

"Really? What does she say? Does she know anything about Maximus and the Ninth Legion?"

"Hang on a minute, I'm just trying to read," said Marcus, laughing.

"This is extraordinary."

"What? What?"

"Flavia says one of Maximus's relatives was the standard-bearer for the Ninth Legion at the time they disappeared. His namesake, Maximus Augustus, no wonder Maximus valued the standard."

"Is she suspicious?"

"No, she simply asks I remember how important it was to him, and should I ever come across it, to ensure it does not fall into the wrong hands, it is to be respected and cherished and not flaunted for political gain or popularity."

"The more I hear of Flavia, the more I like her," said Odell.

"She is a good woman who cared deeply for Maximus and respects his legacy."

"What are you going to do now?"

Marcus did not immediately reply. "I think we should fetch it and place it here in our hut. We will be its custodians and can make sure Tamm is aware of its history. That way, it does not lie rotting in the ground, nor will it fall into the hands of those who will not respect it."

"Maximus would like that very much, Marcus."

"I think he would, but I still wonder how he came to possess it."

"I suspect that's something we will never know, but I'm proud to be a custodian of such an important artefact."

"Indeed."

CHAPTER 13

Present Day:

Harriet sat open-mouthed as she tried to process Ada's words.

"Oh Ada, I'm so sorry, to be the victim of domestic abuse is so tough," she leaned across to place her hands on Ada's.

"I don't like the term victim. I much prefer survivor, I'm not a victim, I'm a survivor."

"Yes, you are, point taken."

"It was a long time ago, I rarely dwell on it now, so much time has passed."

"But when you do, it is still painful?"

"It is, I think what hurts most is the loss of control, the isolation, and the sense of helplessness I felt for such a long time. I often ponder how I let myself get into that situation?"

"I don't think it's something you let yourself get into rather, it's about the controlling actions of another. I don't want to pry, so, please change the subject if you're uncomfortable talking about it."

"Not at all, I experienced the whole gambit of abuse, psychological, emotional, physical, sexual, financial, and what's now called coercive control. He was skilled at that, but in my day, the term did not exist."

"Ada, I don't know what to say," Harriet's voice broke.

"It's fine, I survived, many years have passed, and I can now talk about it without being overwhelmed. I was a librarian in a small town in the Southwest of England, I loved my job, lived with my parents, and had a small group of local friends. Phillip was a friend of my older brother, Andrew. He was five years my senior, good-looking and charming, six foot four, athletic, dark brown hair, large brown eyes, with an engaging smile. My parents thought him a good match, and to be fair, he swept me off my feet. During our courtship, there was never a hint of what was to come, he was attentive, funny, generous, and gregarious. I was utterly in love; how could I have known what I was walking into? For there were absolutely no signs."

"When was it that his behaviour changed?"

"I often think about it, and I suppose it was about a year after we were married. It's hard to remember exactly, there was no eureka moment, I just recall it was little things to begin with, small criticisms of my cooking, or fault found with the cleaning, a crooked picture, a trinket out of place on the mantlepiece. But then, he stopped socialising with me, instead, he would go out with his friends from work, he also made excuses to prevent me from having contact with my family. Before long, he announced I must give up work, we had a huge row about it, he typed and sent a resignation letter in my name. From that moment on, it was my job to look after him and the house, I was no longer permitted access to our money, he gave me a weekly allowance for which I had to present receipts. As the years passed, the allowance became less and less, making it more difficult to make ends meet. Often, he would return from work worse the wear for drink and fly into a rage, it was always the small things that set him off, his dinner was too cold, too hot. Or he found dust on the mantlepiece. He would accuse me of squirreling away the allowance and tell me I'd let myself go; I was ugly and stupid. One of the most hurtful things he did was to burn all the books in the house. It was gradual and, to be honest, it took me a while to understand what was happening, I was in love and wanted to make Philip happy, I thought it was my fault, I Lost my sense of self, my confidence, believed Philip was right."

"But that changed?"

"Yes, the first time he hit me; we had a row about going to Sunday lunch with my parents. He forbade it, I told him I was going, anyway, I remember it so clearly; his face turned a curious red colour, and beads of perspiration formed along his top lip. He walked across and struck me so hard with his fist that I flew into the banister, he broke my left arm."

"Oh my god, Ada!"

"He showed no emotion, no further anger, no remorse, nothing, just picked up his coat from the chair and walked out of the house."

"What did you do?"

"I called a Taxi and went to the hospital."

"Did the hospital question your injury at all?"

"No, dear, I told them I'd fallen."

"The only good thing to come out of it was Philip did not speak to me or cause me further harm for the next two months."

"And then?"

"And then it started again, the next time he hit me, he gave me a black eye and tore out a clump of my hair. I went to the police station, what a waste of time that turned out to be. I made my complaint, but I never heard from them again despite several phone calls to the front desk. And someone, made Philip aware of my visit and as a result, I suffered another beating."

"Ada, I'm so upset to hear that."

"I was incredibly naïve, it was a different age, no one spoke about domestic violence, it was a taboo."

174

"Did you try to speak to your family?"

"Yes, but neither of my parents wanted to listen, it was something you just didn't talk about. They didn't want to hear it. It was the sort of thing that did not happen in nice families. And, my brother Andrew, well, he didn't believe me either, called me a malicious liar to my face."

"Did you ever report Philip again to the police?"

"Yes, on three further occasions, each time, I received a severe beating and additional sanctions, and each time, my complaint went nowhere."

"So, how did you escape?"

"Well, the catalyst, believe it or not, was when Spot entered our lives. He was a mongrel black and white dog; Philip rescued him during some operation at work. Suddenly, I had company. For the first month he lived with us, he cowered under the dining room table. But slowly and surely, he grew in confidence and came out of himself. His unconditional love opened my heart to the possibility of a happier future. Philip had a complicated relationship with him. On the one hand, he was to be fed the best cuts of meat and walked twice daily. He even gave me an allowance for Spots' food! Can you believe it? On the other hand, he completely ignored him. My walks with Spot gave me the space to think; I realised I needed to leave before Philip killed me. He was drinking more heavily than usual, and his violence towards me had intensified.

But how could I get away? I was isolated from my family; the police were unwilling to help; I didn't trust anyone."

"So, what did you do?"

"I played the long game; I worked hard not to enrage Philip. It didn't always work, but it took me a couple of years. I saved Spots' allowance; I'm not proud of myself, but sometimes I fed Philip pies made from tinned dog meat just because I could. It was defiance, or maybe dissent, if you can understand that?" Harriet nodded. "I also bought the cheapest food I could find, past it's best. Slowly but surely, I saved enough for a train ticket. I kept the money under a blanket in Spot's bed. Then I waited until I knew Philip would be at an evening awards presentation. I packed a suitcase, put Spot on his lead, and called a taxi. Even now, I remember the sense of panic. What if he came back unexpectedly? What if the car didn't arrive? I was shaking with fear. I'm not sure if the driver cottoned on, but he charged me a pittance for the journey and kindly carried my suitcase to the platform. I will always be grateful to him. I bought a ticket for the next train, which incidentally terminated at Slough."

"Ada, that was such a brave thing to do."

"It was such a necessary thing to do."

"What happened next? Did Philip come after you? Did he find you?"

"He tried, but he never found me."

"I can believe that."

"I arrived in Slough late at night, I was lucky because while I was in the ladies' toilet at the station, I saw a poster offering accommodation for women with nowhere else to go. And I certainly fell into that category, I rang the number using a nearby payphone. I lived at that hostel for five years, first as a client and then as its manager. It catered for women and children, fleeing violence at home, I was so lucky to find it, it saved my life. Initially, the hostel staff helped me to get a cleaning job at a local pub, they paid me cash in hand, I knew Philip would look for me, so as I got off the train, I changed my name to Ada Brown, and I bided my time. Many interesting characters used to come into that pub, one day, the landlord, William Lamb, took me to one side and asked me if I needed documentation. I must have looked blank, for he laughed loudly before elaborating further. Birth certificate, National Insurance, passport, etc. Then the penny dropped, and I nodded vigorously. With William's help, I created a whole new identity, I will be forever grateful to him."

"What was your original name, if you don't mind my asking?"

"Not at all, I was originally Lucy Robinson then when I married, I became Lucy Russell."

"Ada, your life story is like something from a film!"

"It is a bit, isn't it? Naturally, I understood the women who came to stay in the hostel, common ground if you like, so over time, I made an impact and before long, I was running it."

"You mentioned you stayed there five years, what made you leave?"

"Philip. One day I was in town with the deputy manager when, to my utter horror, I caught sight of him, he was unusually tall and stood out amongst the Saturday crowd. He was walking towards us, scanning the shoppers' faces, Maria had my arm and must have sensed my distress, she immediately steered me into an adjacent charity shop, I stood behind her shaking and crying."

"Oh, my goodness, how terrifying! Did he see you?"

"No, thank God, he walked straight past, but I knew I had to leave."

"How do you think he knew to search for you in Slough?"

"I've thought long and hard about it, he must have realised I fled by train and studied the timetable for the night I left. Perhaps he often walked the streets of Slough looking for me, driven by the outrage he felt at my disappearance and a desire to punish me."

"I never saw him again."

"Do you mind my asking how you ended up living at Fairview?"

"I know what you're thinking, I had a modest lifestyle, how was I able to afford it?"

"Well, not exactly, but it had crossed my mind."

"It's another interesting story, it's true my lifestyle was modest, but I made the most of the money I had and travelled across Europe and further afield when the opportunity arose. One day, ten years after I'd fled, I was sitting attempting to finish a crossword in the Times newspaper when my eye was drawn to a small cryptic headline. *"Spot, the dog's lady owner, could be laughing all the way to the bank."* I only noticed it for two reasons: it was next to the crossword, and, of course, the dog's name stood out for me. I read the article, it was about the lengths Arkwright and Arkwright solicitors from Bristol were going to find Mrs Lucy Russell regarding a sizeable inheritance.

"No?"

"Yes, really, my first instinct was this was a trick, a ruse by Philip to entrap me. So, I did nothing, but it preyed on my mind. After a week, I confided in a close friend who volunteered to make contact and check the validity of the article. It turned out that this newspaper article had been the solicitor's last attempt to contact me. To cut a long story short, Philip had died from a brain aneurysm the year before, he was still married to me, he had no living family, and therefore I stood to benefit. The thing is, not only did I inherit our marital home, but the rest of Philip's sizeable fortune. Thanks to his wealthy parents, I also inherited their country estate, a manor house and one hundred and fifty acres!"

"That's bloody incredible Ada."

"Yes, that's exactly what I thought! After all the pain and anguish I end up with the reprobate's wealth, who'd have thought?" Harriet broke into a smile.

"I'm just wondering if, after you learned of Philip's death, you made contact again with your family?"

"Well, yes, and no, it seems my mother died from pneumonia shortly after I left, my father and brother in a car crash six years later. So, I visited their graves."

"I'm so sorry Ada."

"Don't be, that's the way life goes sometimes, I'm not sure anyway if they were still alive, we could have repaired the damage to our relationship. With the funds I inherited, I set up a shelter for women fleeing domestic violence, I also set up a shelter for men seeking refuge from their violent partners."

"That's amazing, can I ask you something?" Ada nodded. "Are you by any chance the anonymous benefactor paying for Stanley Cross to continue to live at Fairview? "

Ada, simply winked at Harriet, before draining her coffee cup.

"I have a question for you now, is there any word on the syringe and vial I found in the Kitchen bin at Fairview?"

"Expertly side-stepped Ada! No, not yet. But there is a briefing this afternoon, I should know more then."

"What I haven't told you yet is the circumstances in which I came to have the items in my possession. One night, unable to sleep, I went for a walk, I visited the library first and then in the early hours went to Chef's room for a cup of cocoa. I was sitting with my feet on the log burner, when I heard footsteps approaching, I don't know why they bothered me, but they did, and I hastily hid in the broom cupboard."

Harriet noticed, and not for the first time, when Ada was deep in thought, she had an endearing habit, she would run her right index finger backwards and forwards over her lower lip.

"I had the feeling two people entered but, I believe it was a man who walked toward the sink and deposited something in the bin. After they'd gone, I retrieved the vial and syringe. I could not make out what was being said between them, other than a couple of words, 'you fool' and something that sounded like 'detain'. I've gone over and over the events in my mind and I now think the male said D10 not 'detain', D10 was George Moore's room number."

"So, are you saying you think the male was chastising the other person for going to the wrong room?"

"I think it's a distinct possibility, as Vera's room was next to George's."

"Thank you, Ada, I'll take this back to Chief Superintendent Wynn."

"Good, good, now I'm off to check on Ethel, remember, I don't want her prosecuted, the poor woman has had a dreadful life."

"I hear what you're saying, and I will discuss it with the boss, in the meantime, please try to stay out of trouble!" Harriet couldn't help laughing as Ada gave her a dismissive wave. Harriet sat in the canteen for a few minutes more, pondering the extraordinary Ada Brown.

That afternoon, Detective Chief Superintendent Derek Wynn held a briefing with key members of the incident room staff.

"Good afternoon, all, I've asked you here earlier than planned, as there are some developments, I need to bring you up to speed with."

Harriet and Mike Taylor, who were sitting next to each other, exchanged glances.

"Perhaps I can ask DS Paul Jones and Steven Leach to start? "

"Thank you, sir, the results on the syringe and vial recovered by Ada Brown have come back, both tested positive for Fentanyl, and the syringe contained Vera Mortimer's blood. We also recovered a DNA sample from the outside of the vial, it is the results from this, which are unexpected and have caused much debate among us." Said DS Paul Jones.

"Explain please," said Derek Wynn, biting his lower lip.

"The DNA has come back as David Wilson's," at this, many in the room gasped and talked noisily, it fell to Derek Wynn to ask for quiet so Steven Leach could continue his explanation. Harriet grabbed her stomach. "Some of you will be unfamiliar with the Wilsons, but last year, we worked on a job a complex series of killings linked by DNA, one of the victims and two of the killers turned out to be triplets. Two of the three Wilson brothers are deceased, but one, Joe Wilson, remains at large and wanted. The difficulty for us is that David Wilson took his life in prison whilst on remand." The room fell silent until Harriet got to her feet.

"But I think I recall DS Jones explaining to us that whilst the brothers share the same genetic blueprint, which is indistinguishable in a standard DNA test, lifestyle differences can be detected using a more sophisticated test. If I recall correctly, David led a sedentary life and ate a diet of takeaways and junk food, Joe exercised regularly and was an exponent of clean eating. Is it therefore conceivable that the DNA could belong to Joe? And could this be proved scientifically?"

"Bloody Hell Lacey, you do listen! That's right, brilliant recall, I'll get onto this straight away." Said Paul Jones.

"If this is Joe Wilson's DNA, it means he needs to be considered as a person of interest in the suspicious deaths at Fairview," said Derek Wynn.

"To be honest, that makes me very nervous and frankly alarmed. However, as unpalatable as that thought is, I wonder why we are so surprised? His sociopathic profile suggests a need to be noticed, and we already know he likes to play games with the police." Said Harriet.

"Yes, and a word of warning from personal experience; he is a master of charm. If Harriet hadn't recognised his photo and intervened, I may have come to significant harm at his hands." Added Kate Squires.

"Indeed, you're right Kate, we all need to be on our guard." Said Paul Jones.

"Geoff, how are we getting on profiling and talking to Fairview staff?" asked Derek Wynn.

"We are pretty much there; we just need to speak to the last four. They all work permanent night shifts in the medical ward at Fairview. It's proving somewhat tricky to catch up with them."

"I'm more than happy to authorise overtime, catch them just before they start their shifts. We need to finish this piece of work as soon as possible."

"Will do Sir."

"Anything else from Scenes of Crime, Paul, Steven?"

"Yes Sir, Steven carried out some more work on the bite mark on Eileen Graham's arm and he was able to establish the marks are self-inflicted."

"Really? That's good work, Steven, so do we know if Eileen was assaulted?" asked Derek Wynn.

"Having looked at all the evidence, we are of the view that she was not assaulted, she is unwell, sometimes her dementia gets the better of her, in moments of confusion or upset, she throws herself around, self-harms, and sometimes must be restrained for her own safety. Blood tests have established that she has a propensity to bruise easily, the bite marks are hers, and the bruises are consistent with her wrists being held, but not excessively hard." Said Paul Jones.

"Good work. That's one case completed. I will speak to Eileen's son to update him. Mike, are you in a position to report on your interview with Sharon Dean?"

"I am Sir; for a woman who is notorious for her mouthy exchanges, she was remarkably unforthcoming. Indeed, I would say she was terse, especially after she saw the CCTV footage we recorded of her antics. I had prepared myself for a tough interview, but it appears there was no fight left in her. She admitted assaulting Stanley and extorting money from him. I subsequently

charged her with theft and assault. Her partner, Gary Evans, was also arrested

and interviewed. He proved far more talkative and told how Sharon set out to

destroy her stepfather to take all his money, believing it to be rightfully hers,

he admits he went along with it and that he witnessed many of Sharon's

assaults on Stanley, which he now says he very much regrets. We charged him

with theft."

"Another brilliant result. So, Harriet, let's move on to Ethel, shall we?"

"Sir, I am still waiting for her to be well enough to speak to, I will do so

as soon as possible, but there are a couple of pressing matters I would like to

discuss with you regarding Ethel after the briefing."

"Okay, no problem, I think that's everything for now, keep up the good

work and we will meet again tomorrow afternoon at two."

Harriet asked Derek, Mike Taylor, Geoff Harvey, and Kate Squires to stay

behind. Once the room had emptied, she relayed Ada's explanation of how she

came to possess the used syringe and vial, and why Ada believed Vera

Mortimer's death had been a mistake, believing instead the intended victim

had been her love, George Moore.

"I have spoken at length with Ada, and she is adamant she does not

want to prosecute Ethel for her kidnap and incarceration, they seem to have struck up quite the friendship, which leads me to the next matter, according to Ada, something petrified Ethel this morning, as surprising as this is, apparently, it was Sharon Jones who visited the hospital. Ada was by Ethel's side, she says as soon as Sharon entered, Ethel shook so violently Ada had to place a second hand over hers. Suspicious, Ada concocted a story about the doctors, believing Ethel may never speak again. This seemed to satisfy Sharon, who did not hang around, now, I need to speak to Ethel as soon as possible to establish exactly what has gone on, but Ada also pointed out Sharon Jones appears to live a lavish lifestyle. Her clothes are designer, her car is an Aston Martin, her husband is a school caretaker. Whilst there may be a simple explanation for her expensive lifestyle, for example, a large inheritance, it may be prudent to undertake some background research on her."

"If Ada's not careful, she will soon be on our payroll! "Said, Derek Wynn, laughing.

"I know, sometimes it's hard to keep up with her! I was thinking Kate would be the perfect person to investigate Sharon if that's okay with you both?"

"I agree," said, Derek.

"I'd be happy to," replied Kate.

After the meeting, Harriet and Mike ambled back to their cars, "Mike, would you have time to do me a favour?"

"Yes, of course."

"Do you have time for a beer?"

"Always!"

They sat in a corner of 'The Mariner,' a pub within walking distance of Police HQ. Harriet outlined Ada's account of her marriage to Philip Russell. "Please don't think for one minute I don't believe Ada, I do, what is bothering me is the behaviour of the local police, it looks like a closing of ranks, I understand times were different, but I wonder if Philip Russell was also abusive at work, was he a bully? Why did no-one try to help Ada? It's such a long time ago now, it's quite possible no one is left alive who remembers, but would you look into it for me?"

"Of course, I agree it's disturbing, a friend of mine is in the Police Federation of South Gloucestershire. Let me see if he can help."

"Thanks Mike, I'm grateful, Ada is such a life force and has been so helpful with this case."

Just then Harriet's mobile sprang into life, she glanced at the screen to see it was Henry calling her.

"Sorry, Mike, I need to take this."

CHAPTER 14

410 AD Gloucestershire:

The winter of 410 was one of the harshest the settlement had endured, forest ponds frozen for weeks at a time; hoar frosts as thick as snow, bitter winds, sleet, and battering hail. They melted ice over open fires for water and rationed food supplies when they could not hunt, it was a miserable time of aching, empty stomachs and constant thirst. To keep warm and conserve fuel, everyone slept in the long hut, including most of the animals.

One night, just as the guards rotated, the alarm bell clanged, Odell and several of the men leapt to their feet, as they exited the hut, cold air slammed into them with such force it took their breath away. When they reached the gate, they found several guards, including Cassius and Atto, with a prostrate figure at their feet.

"What's going on?" Asked Odell.

"We had just taken up our posts when we heard a strange whimpering sound outside, so we looked through the spyhole to see a dark figure clawing at the gate. Conscious that this could be an ambush, we watched and listened for a few minutes before opening the inner door and dragging the figure into the settlement." said Cassius.

Odell stood astride the figure, who was still moaning face down on the frozen ground, she took the lamp Marcus was holding and waved it backwards and forwards, as she did so, Marcus bent down and rolled the man over.

"Edgar! What in the world are you doing here?" Exclaimed Odell.

Edgar did not immediately reply, he lay on the frozen ground wide-eyed, with a haunted look on his face, Odell repeated her question.
"Vagabonds, help, please," said a hoarse Edgar, before passing out.

Edgar was a mess, a large cut to his face, frostbite on his hands and toes, and deeply cracked lips, he also had a deep wound to his left thigh.

After he'd regained consciousness and warmed up, he spoke once more, gone was the overconfident, sarcastic man of old.

"I know we have not always seen eye to eye, and I do not deserve your help, but I am throwing myself on your mercy, if you can find it in your hearts to help us, I will be your loyal servant till my dying day."

"Steady Edgar," said Odell, suddenly alarmed at his rhetoric.

"Raiders overran our village, tall, hairy, muscular men, well-armed and skilful fighters, the like of which we've never encountered before, they are vicious, with a blood lust. I suppose we 'd become complacent, for we did not see them coming, they have captured all the men and boys, those they haven't killed, are tied up in a nearby open mine. All the women and young children remain in the village for now, anyone who dares to dissent, they kill on the spot. The women and girls are being violated," Edgar's voice faltered, "they raped my wife in front of me, killed my eldest son, for attempting to stand up to them... when, ... I failed to do so." Edgar sobbed and sobbed; Odell placed a hand on his shoulder.

"Enough said, and what of my cousin Alfred?"

"I'm so sorry, he's dead." Odell was silent for a moment or two.

Titus turned to Marcus, "what's that thing Odell does with her finger on her lip?"

Marcus broke into a smile, "she runs her right index finger up and down her lower lip when she's deep in thought."

"I see," said Titus, scrutinising Odell further.

"We will not abandon your village; we leave at dawn." Those gathered stamped their feet and hollered their agreement, except Julius.

"Forgive me, Odell, but he could be feeding us a pack of lies. How do we know we are not about to walk into a trap? Considering your history with this man, why do you believe him so readily?"

"Because Edgar knows full well, death at my hand would be a far worse fate than at the hands of the vagabonds."

As dawn broke, thirty men left the settlement on foot. Conditions were too treacherous to take horses. Felix and Atto remained behind with several teenage boys to guard the fort. Senna, Alwin's partner, was tasked with taking care of Tamm, Ria, Senna's mother, put in charge of Edgar.

The men negotiated the steep climb down from the fort; it was slippery, and thick fog hampered their progress. Eventually, they reached the forest floor. Swiftly and adeptly, Odell led them on. It was not long before they reached the ponds and then turned west, towards the far fringes of the forest. As luck would have it, the fog remained and was still present when they reached the outer edge of the besieged settlement. Although set on a hill, it was a gentle one and not well defended like Odell's home, which was built high up, difficult to reach, and defended with thick walls and deep ditches.

Odell stood amidst her army, "our plan is this, half of you will follow me to the mine to liberate the menfolk, half will go with Marcus to the rear of the settlement, here you will take up strategic positions and await my signal to attack, three owl calls. Once we have reinforcements from the mine, my group will attack from the opposite side. Questions?"

Silence. All knew what Odell expected of them, to fight to the death until one side was victorious.

Odell and Marcus locked eyes, but with no time for shows of affection, Marcus winked, she smiled before turning and running off into the gloom with her men.

"I am confident victory will be ours, my friends." She shouted over her shoulder.

Those guarding the mine entrance were still asleep when their throats were cut, Odell and the others gathered the dead men's weapons and slipped silently into the mouth of a cave, they followed the sounds of snores, coughs, and moans until they came to a large chamber. Here, with the help of lamps, they could see a group of men and boys sitting with their backs to the posts, their hands tied. It was cold; one paltry fire with a dismal flame glowed in the centre of the group.

"Don't be frightened. We are here to help. All I ask is you remain silent for the time being." Said Odell, winking at a small boy who was staring wide-eyed at her. He gave a weak smile in response.

Odell and her men silently set about sorting the prisoners into groups, the elderly, boys who were too young to fight, the injured and the feeble, this resulted in just twenty able-bodied men. Odell recognised one man as a close companion of Alfred's, she had seen him with her cousin many times, he was tall and extremely thin, with lanky limbs and crooked teeth.

"Luti? Isn't it?" she asked.

"Yes, that's right, Odell, thank the gods you've come, how did you hear of our fate?"

"It was Edgar who alerted us."

"What? That cowardly bastard."

"He risked his life to reach us and was near death when he did, he's a broken man."

"Then, I'm grateful to him, what do you need us to do?" asked Luti.

They took those unable to fight into the forest to be collected later, a fire was lit, they huddled around it for warmth.

A short time later, Odell and her troupe arrived at the edge of the village, they lacked weapons, so she instructed they take and use the weapons of fallen enemies and colleagues alike.

From the outset, there was confusion, shouting, and screaming as they roused the enemy. Well trained and organised, they spoke in a tongue none of Odell's men could fathom. It soon became apparent that to make progress, Odell and her fighters would need to work together in pairs or small groups,

Odell and Julius made their way to a rocky outcrop, here they rained down volley after volley of arrows onto the enemy.

Even though they had the element of surprise, it was a frenzied fight, Odell's men fought with courage and valour, but the enemy was well armed, and they were expert fighters. The scene was chaotic and bloody, and the enemies' dirty tricks hampered them. When they set light to some huts, pandemonium broke out and despite their best efforts, some innocents perished in the fires. In the aftermath, it was clear they had paid a high price for freedom. It later came to light the population of Edgar's village was halved.

As they began taking stock and seeing to the injured, Marcus approached, Odell saw him coming and ran across, flinging her arms around him, then she looked him up and down to satisfy herself he was uninjured.

"What are your plans for the survivors? "Marcus asked nuzzling her neck.

"They will come to live with us, they will not survive otherwise, look at them, they are mainly old or very young, so few adults survived."

"And what of our losses?"

"We arrived with thirty men, we return with twenty-five," Odell looked at the ground a quagmire of icy mud and blood.

"It could have been worse, we should thank the gods," said a serious-looking Marcus.

"Have you come across these men before?" asked Odell looking deep into Marcus's eyes.

"That I have, they are fearsome as you saw, I believe they are from a place called Rucia (Russia), a land right on the outermost reaches of the Roman Empire, they speak a tongue I do not know, they are without mercy."

As they were speaking, Odell noticed a small hand weaving its way into hers, she looked down to see the young boy from the cavern looking up at her, he was crying, she bent down and gently lifted him up, holding him in her arms, "shh, don't cry, little one, you are safe now." When the boy ceased crying, Odell handed him to Marcus, who promptly put him on his shoulders, the boy seemed to like this, placing his hands on the top of Marcus's head to steady himself.

Marcus gathered the survivors together in a large circle, Odell stood in the middle, and when their chatter ceased, she stood up straight and took a deep breath.

"Today, we were victorious, the gods were kind to us, but victory comes at a high price, we have lost many who were dearly loved, I find myself grappling with a tough decision and I apologise, but I can see no way you can stay here in your village." A series of cries and wails rang out from the throng.

"As upsetting as it is, the reality is you will die of cold and lack of food, you are also vulnerable to reprisal, look around you, how many men remain standing? How many women of childbearing age? Just a handful, the remainder of you are children or in your twilight years. So, I propose all survivors leave with us and come to live in our settlement, it will be your new home, together, we will be stronger, it is a challenging situation, yes, but we will overcome." Odell's speech was met with subdued silence until a woman about her age stepped forward, of slight frame, wiry like Odell, but shorter with plaited red hair and deep blue eyes.

"My friends and neighbours, Odell, is entirely correct, if we stay in what's left of our beloved village, we will surely die. I know you are grieving the loss of your fathers, mothers, sisters, brothers, and other family members, but we owe it to them to pick ourselves up and find a new life. As obnoxious as Edgar can be, he was savvy enough to recognise the only person who could save us was Odell. We should thank her and her people with all our strength for freeing us. Thank you, Odell, thank you sincerely." The woman took both Odell's hands in hers, as her words sank in, the villagers began to cheer and shout their thanks also.

"It's good to meet you at long last, I've heard so much about you, my name is Banna, Alfred was the father of my children." As she said this her eyes filled with tears, Odell hugged her tight.

"I'm so sorry for your loss, Alfred was always my favourite cousin, have your children survived?" As Odell waited for Banna's response, her stomach churned with nerves.

"The gods were kind, Bel and Cata are over there," she pointed to a boy no older than three and a girl aged about five, holding hands with an elderly man.

"Thank the gods," said Odell with a sigh of relief.

"Everyone, may I have your attention for one last time, just for a minute or two, we shall divide you into small groups, each group will have the help of some of my men. It's important we gather anything that may be of use for example, uneaten and stored food, cooking pots, tools, chickens, pigs, sheep, and horses. Bedding and clothing and any small personal items that have survived. We will load as much as we can onto small carts, and horses, the rest, we will carry. So many have fallen today I suggest we honour the dead by placing them in the village and setting fire to it. The vagabonds will be left to rot in a pit at the edge of the forest. "

There was no dissention to this, the villagers got on with the task in hand, whilst Odell sent Julius and several of the men ahead, the carts would not make it to the settlement gates, so steep was the route, they would need to use a series of pulleys to haul them up and this needed to be organised.

Several hours later, a caravan of villagers and fighters, animals and carts snaked their way through the cold, dank forest. Pockets of fog and rain hampered progress, dripping through the tree canopy. As far as possible, the injured, weak, and young were carried by animal or cart. It began as a subdued journey until the little boy on Marcus's shoulders started to sing. Others joined in, until almost all were singing. This uplift in spirit spurred them on, and they reached the bottom of the settlement hill by dusk. It was a long, arduous process to get everyone and everything to the top, but Odell never gave up, she oversaw the entire process, with a strength of will and legendary bloody mindedness, rarely did she not succeed.

CHAPTER 15

Present Day:

"Henry, how are you? I'm so sorry, we seem to keep missing each other's calls."

"I'm fine, I've been working long tiring hours, but it's worth it, it's so lovely to hear your voice, thank you for all your messages. In my downtime, I've thought a great deal about us."

"Oh, yes? And were these good or bad thoughts?" Asked Harriet.

"Only good thoughts, as far as you are concerned, I know exactly how I feel about you, so, when I come back in a few weeks 'time, I want us to pick up where we left off, if that's okay with you? Life is too short, I've spent far too much time running away from my emotions, I've wasted too much time."

"That would make me so happy, I've not been able to get you out of my mind, to the extent I've had great difficulty concentrating on anything, I won't lie, this separation has been hard, it's made me realise you are the one I want to build a life with, I am ready to move on."

"You don't know how happy I feel, we will talk more next time as I'm due back in surgery. I will try to call you next week, communication is extremely flaky here, however, fingers crossed, I'll be able to get through, stay safe, my love."

"And you, I love you, Henry."

As the call ended, Harriet realised she was quivering, a broad grin spread across her face. Jolted back to the reality of the pub carpark, she giggled loudly before almost skipping across to her car.

That night Harriet could not sleep, thoughts of Henry interrupted her attempts at slumber. Each time he entered her head, she felt a wave of 'joy.' Eventually, at about four, she got up and showered before going downstairs to make coffee. She had an important interview that morning and was determined to be on top of her game and not let Henry enter her head. She made a mental note to tell Ada about her contact with Henry.

At six, she woke Amelia, and had breakfast with her, before setting off to the hospital to speak to Ethel Moore.

Ethel was sitting up in bed swathed in bandages, as Harriet arrived, she was just finishing a liquid breakfast through a straw.

It was impossible to see if she was nervous, if she feared the conversation they were about to have, her bandages disguised it, but Harriet noticed her expansive hands were trembling.

Harriet grabbed a chair and placed it next to the bed. She sat down and took Ethel's hands in hers.

"Ethel, it's okay. I just want to ask you some questions and make sure that you are safe. It would help immensely if you could be honest with me; it will save time. Before we start, I think I should tell you Ada has requested we, the police, take no action against you for her incarceration. I think it's highly likely my boss, Detective Chief Superintendent Wynn, will agree to this."

An enormous sigh emanated from the large patient next to her.

"I suspect you know your attacker and you're frightened to tell me, but I also believe you want to do the right thing. Am I right?"

A muffled "Yes," escaped from the bandages.

"Good, do you feel up to talking?"

"Yes, besides, Ada told me to be truthful. Ada said you are very good at your job and would give me no peace until I tell you everything," said a hoarse Ethel.

"Oh, Ada did, did she?" Harriet suppressed a giggle and gave Ethel's hand a squeeze. "Because this is a serious matter, I must caution you before we continue: '*Ethel, you do not have to say anything, but it may harm your defence if you do not mention when questioned something which you later rely* on in court, anything you do say may be given in evidence.' Do you understand this?"

"Oh yes, dear, Ada went through it with me."

"Okay then, the night we found Ada, before the attack on you, you came to see me in Mrs Pritchard's office, you were upset, and when I asked you what was wrong, you said, and I quote, 'I knew something was amiss, but I was complicit, I turned a blind eye, I should have spoken out sooner.'"

"Yes, I was in quite a state that night. I'd been drinking vodka, you see."

"But you knew what you were doing?"

"Oh, yes, dear, unfortunately, I knew only too well."

"What was it you wanted to tell me that night? What was it you were going to tell me?"

There was a pause; Harriet assumed this was while Ethel gathered her thoughts. Her hands shook once more; Harriet gave them a squeeze.

"I had such anger in me, such hurt feelings. I know the difference between right and wrong and I knew I'd crossed a line. My silence was eating me up. The nightly cocoa was being tampered with and I said nothing."

"How did you know and in what way was it being tampered with?" asked Harriet gently.

"I saw it being tampered with, one night I entered the kitchen as usual to fetch the cocoa, as I turned the corner, I saw someone leaning over the trolly, I was suspicious, so I quietly re-traced my steps and then coughed loudly as I again entered the kitchen. The person at the trolley nearly jumped out of their skin, I saw a spoon in their hand, which they'd been using to crush several tablets in a bowl. The person passed the tablets off as vitamins, said they were to be added to the cocoa, they then calmly continued to add them to the two thermos jugs stirring as they went."

"Did you know the tablets weren't vitamins, or did you just suspect?"

"It didn't take a genius to work it out, especially when I heard about missing personal items from residents' rooms."

"Was this the work of one person or more?"

"Two of them were at it, working as a team, one of them threatened me, told me that I would be blamed if I opened my mouth."

"Why didn't you tell someone?"

"Mainly for stupid family loyalty."

"Sorry, Ethel, I don't understand, are you saying one of those involved is related to you?"

"Yes."

"I know it's really hard for you to tell me their names, but I need to know."

"I know, Ada said I'd feel so much better about myself if I did and she said it would end the coercion, be safer for me in the long run."

"Wise words."

"So, the person putting the ground tablets in the cocoa was Matron."

"Alice Goodman?"

"Yep, but she was under the thumb of my niece, she's the brains behind the operation. Everyone thinks she's perfect, she's the most popular member of staff, she comes across as respectful, professional, kind. But she's a huge spoilt bitch who's only interested in money, designer gear and social climbing. She's been cruel to me, unkind, she calls me her fat, ugly aunt, she made me feel like I didn't deserve my job. Sometimes she slaps me for no reason, and delights in telling me the residents think I'm a crude, unpleasant hag." Harriet could hear the emotion in Ethel's voice and patted her hand.

"Alice would put drugs in the cocoa, and the other one would work late and take items of jewellery from unconscious residents for Alice to sell, although not all were sold."

"Do you know where Alice took the items to sell?"

"Nope, sorry."

"That's fine."

"And the other one's name is?" There was a long pause.

"Sharon Jones."

Harriet took a sharp intake of breath, "and she's your niece?" Ethel nodded. "I remember the night we found Ada, Sharon came to tell me Ada wished to speak to me, just as you were leaving, I remember you locked eyes."

"Well yes, she never liked me, saw me as an embarrassment. I'm the rough side of the family as far as she's concerned, the only member of that side of the family left now."

"Ethel, you are doing so well, I know it's hard for you, but do you think you could tell me who attacked you?"

Ethel was silent.

"Would it help if I told you that I suspect it was Sharon?"
Ethel began to shake all over, and rock backwards and forwards, deep sobs were audible from beneath the bandages, Harriet leaned in towards her.

"It's okay Ethel, please, you are safe here, there's a police officer guarding the door to your room, I promise you I will do everything in my power to make sure whoever did this to you spends many, many years in prison."

After what seemed like many minutes, Ethel spoke. "You thought right."

"It was Sharon Jones?"

"Yep."

"Thank you, Ethel, I know how hard that was for you."

"When she realises, I've told you she will stop at nothing to silence me," Harriet gave Ethel's hands another pat. "There's something else as well, there is another person involved, but I don't know who they are." Said Ethel quietly.

"Really?"

"I overheard Sharon speaking to them on the phone one day in the garden, they were clearly arguing over the division of the spoils, I heard Sharon threaten she'd cut them off but, I know only that."

"Okay, thank you Ethel, you've done so well, you must be tired now, I may come back and see you another time, if that's okay?"

Ethel nodded.

As Harriet tidied away her notes, the door swung open to reveal Ada with several other Fairview residents pushing a trolley containing fine china cups and saucers, plates of cakes and biscuits, and cafetieres.
"Ethel, I've had a word with the doctor who says you can try a piece of Mr Aubert's Victoria sponge, but only if he can have a slice too! There's a nurse coming in a minute to remove some of your bandages." Ethel clapped her hands together as Ada winked at Harriet.

"Ethel, I shall leave you in the capable hands of your friends. Thank you for your honesty."

A few days later, Derek Wynn called a briefing, which proved to be quite a lively affair. The first revelation came from Steven Leach. Apparently, the partial footprint found in the blood on the floor of Ethel's room was a match for a pair of shoes seized from Sharon Jones. Sharon had been arrested for the assault on Ethel Moore and the theft of resident's jewellery. Derek Wynn had given Geoff Harvey the task of interviewing her.

"Geoff, are you in a position to update us regarding your interviews with Sharon Jones?" asked Derek Wynn.

"Yes Sir, there's not much to tell. She's refusing to answer questions. Alice Goodman, however, is singing like a canary and, as a result, has fully implicated Sharon in the drugging of residents and theft of their jewellery. I think I should clarify when I say the drugging of residents, I mean crushed tablets in their cocoa."

"Good work Geoff."

"Geoff, have you asked Alice about the one member of staff you've not been able to track down yet? And have you got any further with your enquiries into the whistle-blower?" asked Harriet.

"She's strangely noncommittal, but I'm on it. We are currently searching her office. I'll let you know if we find anything of interest. When I mentioned the whistle-blower in interview, she turned extremely pale, saying she didn't know their identity, but I don't think she's telling the truth. I want to see if we turn up anything useful in her office before broaching the subject again."

Later that day, Harriet gathered a few of the detectives working on the case together. Joe Wilson had been playing on her mind, he was a dangerous individual, and she felt sure he was one step ahead of them, it was her view that they must come up with a strategy for finding and dealing with him before he turned his attention to another resident or one of her colleagues got hurt, or worse.

It was a select group who gathered in Harriet's kitchen that evening, an inner circle of trusted colleagues. First to arrive, Kate Squires and Steven Leach, as Harriet welcomed them, she noticed a glow to Kate and intimacy between the two, although she wouldn't have put them together, they did work as a couple, intrigued, she made a mental note to ask questions of Kate later. Next, Paul Jones and Mike Taylor appeared, both clutching bottles of wine. Then Derek Wynn and Geoff Harvey arrived, both clutching flowers. As Harriet poured drinks for everyone, she reflected on how good it felt to be hosting her friends.

They ate olives, breadsticks, and antipasti before Harriet produced several large home-made pizzas. Suitably full, talk turned from food and gossip to work.

"Everyone, I have to confess to having an agenda when I invited you all here tonight," said a smiling Harriet.

"I knew it! " Mike Taylor playfully slammed his fist onto the table.

"Well, I for one don't mind, that was exceptional, thank you, Harriet, now what's on your mind?" Asked Derek Wynn.

"I have a growing sense of unease regarding Joe Wilson, I know we haven't yet definitively established his involvement in this case, but my gut is telling me he's fully immersed in Fairview, and we need to be extremely careful. There's no doubt he is a clever and accomplished manipulator, and let's not forget he's also wanted for murder. It's my view that we need to come up with a plan to locate and detain him, I also think the fewer staff involved, the better."

"I couldn't agree with you more, from a scientific point of view we are struggling to place Joe in Fairview. The DNA sample recovered by Ada is microscopic, it's difficult to draw definitive conclusions from it. But, as unscientific as this sounds, it's my gut feeling too he's been there in some capacity." Said Paul Jones.

"I'd just like to add that we confirmed this afternoon the levels of injected fentanyl found in Major Moore and Vera Mortimer were fatal, no doubt about it, the ingested tablets in the cocoa induced drowsiness, nothing more, but the quantity of the injected drug sufficed to kill each recipient several times over." Said Steven Leach.

"That's really chilling," said Harriet, pulling a face.

"Indeed, our task now is to establish who else, if anyone, may have fallen victim to the same fate." Replied Paul Jones.

"And we think the motive is what?" Asked Derek Wynn.

"I'd say on balance, it was probably greed, Ethel overheard Sharon Jones arguing with someone on the phone, the conversation appeared to be about the division of spoils, I'm guessing they were discussing stolen jewellery." Said Harriet.

"That may be part of it, but I think there is more to Joe Wilson than that, he'll have another angle, I'm sure," said Mike.

"I'm sure you're right, but I've no clue what that might be, anyone else?" Asked Harriet, no one replied.

"My team have been working nights for the last week, two of the four staff were still outstanding, then tonight, just before I arrived, I learned the missing two are agency staff, that had not been taken off the books. Apparently, they have not worked there for over eighteen months. I have, of course, asked for this to be verified and for the two individuals to be interviewed." Said Geoff Harvey.

"Oh, my God! Does this mean that the two we are looking for are staff we have already spoken to and checked, and are still working at Fairview?" Asked a wide-eyed Kate Squires.

"Potentially yes," said a grim-looking Derek Wynn.

"The whole situation is a fucking mess, if you will excuse my French," said Mike before continuing, "I think it's fair to say Joe Wilson has been one step ahead of us from the start and I, for one, don't like that one bit, it's time to turn the tables."

"I agree, we need a plan, and fast," said Derek Wynn, shaking his head.

"I think I may have an idea," said Harriet, in a whisper."

CHAPTER 16

412 AD Gloucestershire:

Harvest time was traditionally demanding, long hours, physical, dusty work, the whole settlement expected to play its part from the youngest to the oldest. The crops had to be cut, gathered, and brought in from the fields, the seed-heads beaten from their stalks; the grain sorted and stored before the autumn storms. As luck would have it, this harvest saw only dry and sunny weather. Marcus oversaw each element and for the first time, Tamm and Atto, the little boy Odell and Marcus rescued from the mine, worked alongside them. At six and seven years of age respectively, they were sometimes a hindrance, but Marcus took it in his stride, with good humour.

Odell had just returned from a successful hunting trip with her brother Alwin and Julius, when a hay-cart trundled around the corner into the main square, on top were Marcus, Tamm, and little Atto, as he had become known, for Alwin's best friend was also called Atto. They were waving wildly, Odell laughed and waved back, what a beautiful family I have, she said to herself.

"Marcus, Marcus, can you spare a moment?" shouted adult Atto as he approached.

"What's up?"

"There's a female at the gate asking for you."

"There is?" Said Marcus, his eyebrows raised, "what does she look like?"

"It's hard to say, she's dressed in traditional Roman clothing; a hood obscures her head," Atto replied.

"Have you asked her business?" Said Marcus.

"Yes, she declined to talk to anyone other than Marcus Atilius."

Marcus jumped down from the hay cart and reached up to catch the boys, one by one, he gently placed them on the ground next to their mother, winking at her as he did so.

"I think you'd better see what this woman wants with you," said Odell smiling, but inside, her stomach churned. What could this woman's business be with Marcus? And why did it bother her so much?

"Come on boys, let's see what's going on at the gate," Odell's curiosity had got the better of her, taking the boys by the hand, she led them towards the front of the settlement. She arrived in time to see a woman remove her hood and embrace Marcus.

"Marcus Atilius, you look well, it's good to see you, my old friend."

"And you, Flavia Augustus, I'm impressed by your mastery of the local tongue. To what do we owe this visit?"

"I've come to see the place and people who captured Maximus's heart."

Odell knew what she really meant; she'd come to see Odell for herself, she placed a hand on her chest, had she come to cause trouble? What did she want? Odell moved a little closer.

Flavia was breathtakingly beautiful, a little taller than she was, with a tiny waist, slender figure, oval face, large green eyes, long dark eyelashes, straight nose, dark red lips, and jet-black hair twisted and pinned on top of her head.

"Flavia, I'd like you to meet Odell, she is the most important person in my life and the head of our settlement," said Marcus, holding out his hand to Odell. Odell took his hand, she smiled and bowed towards Flavia. "Welcome to our home, Flavia, will you and your men stay the night and join us in celebrating the completion of the harvest?" Flavia's gaze was direct, but not overtly unfriendly.

"It would be an honour, Odell, I look forward to making your acquaintance properly later, for I have heard much about you." Odell scrutinised her face for signs of hostility, but if she felt any, it wasn't on show, not yet anyway. Just then, Tamm and little Atto came into view.

Flavia's right hand shot to her throat, and she reddened, "oh, my goodness, oh, I didn't know, Marcus, why did you not tell me?"

"Tell you what, Flavia?" Asked Marcus with a blank look on his face.

"That I have a son?"

"Sorry, What?"

"That little boy before us is my husband's boy, no doubt about it; he's the spitting image of him."

"You are correct, Tamm is Maximus's son, but he is also my son," said Odell, sounding far calmer than she felt.

"Let me show you to the guest hut; we can talk later when you have rested," said Marcus, seizing the initiative.

Several hours later, Marcus and Odell were in their hut preparing to join the evening celebrations.

"Marcus, I'm worried, worried Flavia will try to take Tamm away from us." Marcus spun around to look at her.

"I like Flavia. She would not do such a thing. I'm sure it was just the shock of discovering her husband had fathered a child that made her say what she did." His demeanour did not reassure Odell.

"She is powerful and beautiful and clearly used to getting her way. I can't compete."

Marcus walked across and embraced Odell. "You have just described yourself, my love. Your beauty is renown, your long curly dark brown hair, blue eyes, dark arching eyebrows, plump full lips, and disarming smile. You also are the leader of this settlement and by the way, when have you ever let anyone, anyone, walk all over you? And one other thing, you have a true heart, a kind spirit." Odell nuzzled her head into Marcus's chest.

"I love you, Marcus Atilius; the moment I set eyes on you toiling to keep your fellow soldiers warm, I loved you. I love you for your generosity towards others. You are a good man who does the right thing; you are loyal and respectful and caring and the bravest soldier I've ever encountered. I also think you are one of the most beautiful men I have ever set eyes on, and what happened with Maximus was a moment in time, it was never about love."

"I know that."

"You do?"

"I've always known it," Odell sighed with relief, all those years of guilt, of wanting but not knowing how to tell Marcus, and he knew all along.

The harvest celebrations went on late into the night with no hint of discourse from Flavia, who was the perfect guest, but Odell could not dispel a sense of foreboding. Odell, Flavia, and Marcus chatted into the early hours. Flavia had many questions about how the soldiers had come to live in the settlement, about their attempts to find their commander, how it had taken them so long to return home. But at no point did she ask about Odell's relationship with her husband, much to Odell's relief.

The next day, Odell offered to take Flavia to the place she first came across Maximus and his soldiers. Marcus suggested he accompany them, but both women insisted they would rather go alone.

It was not until they reached the ridge where Odell had first glimpsed the Romans that Flavia spoke.

"Did you love my husband, Odell?" Taken aback by Flavia's directness, Odell did not immediately reply.

"I cared for him, he was a good man and a good friend, I suppose there was an attraction between us, but no, I did not love him."

"Did you know he was in love with you?"

"Only when he told me so, and it troubled me, for by then I had strong feelings for another."

"Marcus?"

"Yes, but neither of them knew at that time."

"How did you come to lie with my husband?"

"Do you think knowing will make it any less painful?" Asked Odell.

"Please just indulge me."

"We were on our way back from Corinium when we were ambushed by a group of men. We found ourselves in a fight for our lives, when the biggest man of the group dropped Maximus to the ground, I ran at the brute and jumped onto his back. I kicked him in the ribs, but I fell and hit my head, I was out cold, apparently, my actions bought Maximus enough time to get back onto his feet and thrust his sword into the man. When I awoke, we were on our way back home, in a campsite outside Glevum. I have thought about the moment many times, analysed it, the best I can come up with is I was overcome with a mixture of survivors' relief and a rush of adrenalin. In my defence, I did not know Maximus was spoken for."

"Would it have made a difference?"

"It would have made all the difference."

"He never told you he was married?"

"Not until later."

"Thank you, Odell, I wish you no ill will, I have my own money and status and now I have the truth, I think I'm ready to rebuild my life. My family and Maximus's family believe I worshipped Maximus, I did not, he had his faults as we all do, he could be selfish and impulsive, and he gave up too easily. Would our marriage have lasted even without you? I doubt it, we both wanted very different things. Maximus's family is entitled and rich, if they knew of Tamm's existence, they would surely insist he's brought back to Rome, I'm not going to tell them."

"Oh Flavia, thank you, I never meant to cause you harm."

"You didn't Odell, Maximus did." Odell flung her arms around Flavia.

"Can I tell you a secret Odell?"

"If you'd like to."

"I have strong feelings for a man in my employ, a former Gladiator called Spiculus, I cannot help myself; he is always in my thoughts and when in my presence, my knees feel as if they will fold beneath me, I cannot keep my eyes from him. I'm minded to leave my home and start a new life with him, just as you have with Marcus."

"I believe you deserve happiness Flavia, go, and find your man, and live your life the way you see fit."

"Thank you, that means a lot."

"Do you want to turn back, or would you like to see the camp?" Asked Odell.

"I would like to see it very much, one last thing, be wary of my armed escort, I have a feeling some are loyal to Maximus's father. I fear I have left you with a problem by coming, for I know they will tell him of Tamm's existence."

"I'm glad we've met; I'm not frightened of Maximus's father or his men."

"I'm not sure there's anything you fear!" Said Flavia smiling.

"Bears." Said Odell laughing.

With that, the two women wandered around the ruins of the old camp, exploring the site, and examining the overgrown part-built road. Odell even showed Flavia the hiding place where she discovered the eagle standard, she did not however, mention its existence, but gave Flavia the remaining items still concealed in a leather pouch inside, an ornate dagger, and several gold rings.

In some ways Odell was sad to see Flavia leave a week later, she knew she would not see her again, but she would not forget her.

No one noticed Tamm was not with little Atto until lunchtime. Marcus had left them sorting grains in one of the barns, he had meant to check on them, but a wheel came off one of the carts and had to be repaired, and it was a couple of hours before he found little Atto. Someone had tied the poor mite up in the barn, he was tearful with frustration for he'd been unable to come to Tamm's aid, they were completely dedicated to one another. The first Odell knew something was wrong was when she heard Marcus cry out, she turned to see him running out of the barn with Atto under one arm.

"I'm going to kill her; I'm going to kill her," he raved.

"Slow down, what's happened?"

"Flavia has taken Tamm." Odell did not believe for one minute; Flavia would turn on them like that.

"I'm not so sure, she told me she had no intention of taking him and I believed her. She did, however, warn me some of her escort might be loyal to Maximus's father."

"We need to stop them, all of them, otherwise we will never be free from attempts to take him," Marcus's voice cracked. "I love that little boy as my own, I could not bear to lose him."

"I know, we will take a group of our best men and cut them off before they reach the main road to the port, come, we must hurry," said Odell.

It was a group of fifteen who ran out of the settlement and almost slid down the hillside, such was their haste. At the bottom, Odell led them at pace through the undergrowth, deftly darting along deer tracks until they reached the ponds, then onwards towards the westernmost edge of the forest. Local knowledge was on their side, and it wasn't long before they picked up a trail of horse hooves on the forest floor, as they turned a corner to a clearing, they could see Flavia and her men in the distance. There seemed to be some type of argument occurring, one man held Tamm by the shoulders. Odell gestured to her men to drop to the ground and move in closer, using the cover of the undergrowth.

"Marcus, you need to translate for me, I don't understand what they're shouting," whispered Odell.

"Flavia is telling some of the soldiers they are traitors, she says she gave her word Tamm would remain with his mother, she is threatening to have them all flogged, but they don't seem too concerned, it seems I misjudged her, oh."

"Oh, what? Marcus?" Asked Odell.

"Flavia has produced a dagger, she is brandishing it at the ringleader, she's feisty and agile, she's taken out one, no two of the escort, oh no, the dagger has been seized from her, she is being restrained, those loyal to her are fighting, but they are all injured."

"I think it's time we stepped in."

Marcus didn't need to be told twice; he ran full pelt into the group. By the time Odell and the others arrived; the traitors were dead, and Marcus was embracing Tamm.

"Thank goodness you came. I'm so sorry, this was not my doing," said Flavia.

"I know," said Marcus, kissing Tamm and holding him close.

"Thank goodness you're safe," said Odell.

"Thank you, but I don't quite know how I'm going to get home now."
Odell's index finger caressed her lower lip.

"Odell, we can take Flavia. We know the way," said Felix, pointing to
Cassius and Titus. "And we were Maximus's friends, so his family won't be
suspicious. Flavia's injured escorts can follow when they've recovered."

"Are you sure? All of you?" They nodded, "then there isn't much time.
Ride hard to catch the boat, thank you. Safe journey, Flavia, and good luck,"
said Odell.

Odell hugged Tamm and took Marcus by the arm as she watched
Maximus's wife disappear through the trees.

"Hurry back, you three, we need you and we will miss you," she shouted
after them. They waved back.

CHAPTER 17

Present Day:

The following day, Harriet arrived at Fairview just before 9.am and made her way to Mrs Pritchard's office. The General Manager was visible through the glass door, pacing up and down, wisps of bleached hair escaping from her usually tidy bun, and she looked thinner than when Harriet had last seen her. Knocking on the door, but not waiting for a response, Harriet entered.

"You'll wear a hole in the carpet if you're not careful, Rita."

"Och, I know, but I find myself out of sorts, I offered my resignation to Mr Hinchcliffe, but he's declined to take it, I'm trying to work out if I am to blame for this mess the buck must stop with someone." It struck Harriet how pale and opaque Rita's face looked.

"I don't think you should be too harsh on yourself. What's been happening here is as far from normal as it's possible to get. I would say there's a need for continuity, so please stay." Harriet gently placed a hand on Rita's arm.

Rita managed the merest of smiles as she gestured to Harriet to take a seat.

"There's a new deputy manager and a new matron arriving later this morning, which should help. I'm just waiting for the agency to confirm their details. Ethel is likely to be discharged from the hospital at the end of the week. I am more than happy to nurse her here. Her rooms have been prepared for her."

"That's really kind. Do you mind my asking if there's a future for Ethel here?"

"Absolutely, Ada has filled me in on the gory details. The way Sharon Jones treated her is unforgivable. I'm not unsympathetic to the situation she found herself in. What Ethel did was the act of a desperate woman. Who knows how any of us might behave under similar circumstances? If she wants her old job back, she is most welcome to it."

"That's very generous of you and good to hear, it seems she has become firm friends with Ada and some of the other ladies, I think you will find a wholly changed woman."

"Yes, so I understand, I'm sure Ada Brown will be the death of me! She's such a force of nature."

"She is indeed, but she has also lived through poverty and some traumatic times in her life."

"I did not know that, I assumed wrongly; she was born with a silver spoon in her mouth," said Rita frowning.

"Far from it, she has survived much physical and psychological harm and despite this, her natural kindness and empathy has remained intact."

"I shall look at her in a different light from now on."

On the Friday of the following week, Harriet had just entered Fairview's main hallway, when she heard laughter and raised voices coming from the blue sitting room. Her curiosity piqued, she walked towards the door, which was ajar, inside, she saw Ada, Ada's carer Linda, Maude Berry, and Stanley Cross, plus some other residents, they were gathered around someone, she couldn't see who, but they were in a wheelchair. Harriet entered and was immediately spotted by Ada.

"Harriet dear, you are just in time to see our transformation," she stood to the side, and there in their midst was a beaming and almost unrecognisable Ethel. She was wearing a smart pair of tailored navy trousers and a wine-coloured blouse with a neck scarf, on her feet, a pair of black ankle boots, gone was the auburn straight hair plastered to her head, in Its place, a smart natural short pixie cut, it suited her immensely, thought Harriet. Someone had even covered her nasty facial scarring with a light concealer.

"Oh, my goodness Ethel, it's so good to see you, you look fabulous." Harriet walked across and hugged her.

"I feel a million dollars, never did I think my life would change so, I am so grateful to everyone, I cannot begin to tell you." Gone was the socially awkward angry woman.

"Well, young lady, I think that's quite enough excitement for one morning, please allow me to wheel you back to your room," said Stanley Cross with a spring in his step, winking at Ethel he took control of her chair. The sound of someone shouting Ada's name from the hallway interrupted the moment, Ada exited the room and found Rita Pritchard on the other side of the door, with her hands on her hips.

"Ah, there you are, what pray have you been up to in there?"

"Lovely to see you too Rita," said Ada, walking towards her, "we've been welcoming Ethel back and I think you'll agree our makeover was most successful." Out of the sitting room came Stanley, pushing Ethel.

"Goodness me, welcome back Ethel, you look …."

"Beautiful," said Ada.

"No, I was going to say 'bonny', I'm so pleased you are here," said a smiling Rita. "Is this your work Ada?"

"Team effort Rita, team effort."

"Good work everyone, really good work, now Ada, I'd like to see you in my office if you'd be so kind?"

"I wonder what I've done this time?" Ada whispered to Harriet.

"No idea, but I shouldn't keep her waiting," Harriet winked at her friend.

Ada entered the General Managers office, "please have a seat, Ada," Rita sat down behind her Victorian desk.

"Right, I've thought long and hard and I've decided there need to be some changes around here, despite my best efforts, things have got out of hand, and I cannot afford for this to happen again. It seems Mr Hinchcliffe believes in me and has asked that I stay on, I have only agreed to do so if I can implement change."

"I'm not sure I like where this is going," said Ada under her breath.

"Now Ada, I know we haven't always seen eye to eye, and in the past, I accept I may have been a little hard on you, there is a new job role available within Fairview, for which there is only one person remotely suitable."

"Okay, but I have no idea what you are talking about Rita."

"I need you, Ada, I need you to run all the activities within Fairview, if you're willing to take up the challenge? For you seem to instinctively know what the residents want, what they are feeling and how to keep everyone happy, what do you say?" There was silence for a moment or two.

"Rita, I'm rarely rendered speechless, but this is one such occasion, let me just ask a few questions before I commit myself, if I may?"

"Of course, fire away."

"When you say I'll be in charge of activities, you actually mean I must run all my ideas and plans past you?"

"No, I mean, you will have carte blanche to arrange what you like so long as it falls within health and safety rules and the set budget, which I have to say I think you'll find generous at £15,000 annually." Ada took a sharp intake of breath, already her brain was whirring with the possibilities such money would bring.

"So, If I wanted to get a hairdresser in once a week, and a beautician, you wouldn't have any objections?"

"Not at all."

"Pilates, and yoga, and meditation classes?"

"Fill your boots."

"Okay, but what if I wanted to organise a Ceilidh dance complete with kilts, haggis, and whisky?"

"Sounds fun."

"What about 'life drawing' in the drawing room?"

"How about the Library?"

"Yes, yes, I will take it on with pleasure," said Ada, laughing.

"Thank you, Ada. I appreciate your support more than you will ever know."

Harriet found Mike in the beer garden of 'The Mariner' there was a glass of white wine waiting for her.

"Hello, you, apologies for being a little late," said Harriet.

"No problem. I've been enjoying the spring sunshine."

"Yes, it's beautiful." Harriet raised her head and closed her eyes for a minute to take in the sun's warmth.

"I promised to report back re my enquiries into Ada's past, and it turns out to be every bit as interesting as she is," said Mike.

"I'm so intrigued. What did you find?"

"I owe a debt of gratitude to my friend in the Police Federation, Lewis Smith, he searched back through records and enlisted the help of retired police officer David Bryant, who served his probation at Greenlane Police Station at the time Ada's husband Philip Russell was the Inspector there. What is more surprising, no, that's not the right word, astonishing, is that it turns out he was on the front desk the first time Ada, or rather Lucy as she was then, came in to make a complaint about Philip. David recalled the grace, the poise with which she explained what had happened to her despite sickening injuries to her face, and he remembered she told him it wasn't the first time this had happened, she described the time her husband broke her left arm. Horrified by this, he immediately went to his sergeant, who came to the front desk and spoke to Lucy, but David recalls after this,things suddenly changed. He thinks the sergeant made the connection to Philip Russell. Lucy was told they would be in contact, but as far as he knows, this never happened. He witnessed the sergeant shred Lucy's written complaint, David Bryant found himself in Philip Russell's office, where he was told to mind his own business, he remembers Philip went to great lengths to paint Lucy as mentally unstable and clumsy, told him she was always walking into things. This was not the impression David had of her. He also left David with no illusions his career depended on staying quiet about Lucy's complaint; to this day, David bitterly regrets his silence. I recorded what he said."

"It is my one great regret I did not find the courage to stand up for that young woman, that I allowed myself to be manipulated and silenced, on reflection, I was new, I did not know how to raise the matter further, but I should have found the strength to help her. I would very much like to apologise to Lucy for my inaction all those years ago, to ask for her forgiveness."

"Poor David, it was a different time," said Harriet.

"Yes, it was, you know that from your work on the domestic violence unit."

"I do, in Ada's day there were almost no domestic violence services, no specialist laws, and no counselling, you didn't leave your husband or partner, it just wasn't done, it just wasn't an option."

"That is so depressing, it must have been hell for many women."

"It was, and for some men, who suffered at the hands of their wives or partners."

"Indeed, now, I believe you said Lucy made further complaints to the police?"

"Yes, three, she told me on each occasion she complained she received a further beating."

"We could not find further documented evidence of two of the complaints, I suspect they were also brushed under the carpet, and unlikely to have been recorded, But David tracked down one further officer who, like him, was on the front desk when Lucy came to complain about her husband. This officer, Greg Myles, had a similar experience to David, Philip Russell made it very clear to him the complaint would go nowhere, this officer was so upset he made a pocketbook entry, had to make it in code to hide it from his sergeant. He kept that pocketbook when he retired, I have a photocopy of part of the entry."

"No? What does it say?"

"At 1530hrs on Saturday 23rd January 1965, a woman I now know to be Lucy Russell attended the front desk at Greenlane police station.... I saw her left eye socket was black and swollen, the left side of her cheek swollen and the left side of her lip cut. I contemporaneously took down her complaint of domestic assault...... she identified her assailant as a Philip Russell... I found Lucy to be forthright and articulate. I took the complaint to Sergeant Frank Bell as the assailant was identified as our station Inspector. Later in my shift I was summonsed to Inspector Philip Russell's office, also present was Sergeant Bell, Inspector Russell thanked me for taking his wife's complaint, then described her as mentally unstable and claimed she was in the habit of injuring herself for attention, he told me there would be no further action and I was not to discuss the matter with my colleagues to maintain his wife's reputation."

"Mike that's incredible, the man was a monster."

"Philip Russell had a reputation for being a brute but, he could also turn on the charm. We found documented complaints against him for violence, made by both police officers and members of the public, but they were all recorded as unsubstantiated. He was clearly skilled at extricating himself from difficult situations, we are talking about a time when there was no CCTV, no mobile phones, no computers. It was often one word against another. Philip

Russell intimidated officers to cover for him, I spoke to two former officers who served with him, who wish to remain anonymous, but who confirmed he blackmailed them to deny his involvement in assaults.

"What a repulsive individual."

"He really was a complete bastard, his ability to switch on the charm, however, fooled his senior officers, what was allowed to go on in Greenland Police Station was a scandal, senior officers must have heard the rumours, yet they failed to carry out due diligence in my opinion."

"I completely agree, did you find out anything else?"

"I did, but I must warn you it is distressing, and as far as I know, Ada did not mention it to you. You know, there's always a chance that she may take offence at us looking into her background?"

"I suppose you're right and that's the last thing I want, it's just I found her story so compelling, I wanted to know if it could be corroborated, I don't know Ada extremely well, but well enough to believe that validation of what happened matters very much to her."

"Well, we certainly have that, the local cottage hospital records were kept in large leather-bound books, when it closed in the 1970's, these were preserved. Lewis Smith found them in the federation archives amongst similar ledgers from the local prison. It's extraordinary they have survived, clearly someone at the time saw fit to rescue them, anyway, there are two entries in the hospital ledgers regarding Lucy, the first, records her broken left arm, the second is several years later, it records severe bruising to Lucy's stomach and the subsequent miscarriage of a baby boy."

CHAPTER 18

413AD Gloucestershire:

Three long, harsh winter months passed before the settlement saw Felix, Cassius, and Titus return. Early one morning, Odell noticed a commotion at the front gate, grabbing her bow she ran towards the ruckus, being careful not to slip on the icy ground. Alwin was in the watch tower shouting to someone below.

"Alwin, what's going on?" Yelled Odell.

"Felix, Titus, and Cassius are on foot and running towards us, but they are being pursued, I can hear horses' hooves and men shouting in the distance, I've sent a group of our men to help them."

"Good, now sound the alarm, where's Marcus do you know?"

"I'm here," what's going on?"

"It seems Felix, Cassius and Titus are being pursued, hunted down, they are trying to make it back to us, Alwin has sent out a party to meet them."

"I see, good, I'll make sure the women, children and elderly make their way to the long hut and then come back to join you," Odell nodded her agreement.

A little less than ten minutes later, a bedraggled and breathless trio threw themselves through the open gate, the heavy doors slammed behind them. An eery silence as everyone craned for sounds of their pursuers, then the unmistakable hiss of air borne arrows, luckily, none hit their intended targets, after that, no further resistance. Clearly, the pursuers thought better of attacking a fortified settlement.

Once the trio had washed and had their wounds tended to, they joined Odell and Marcus in the long hut, here they hungrily tucked into a thick soup eaten with large hunks of bread. Marcus made sure they had plenty of home-made ale, but not so much as to render them unable to tell their tale. They looked a sorry state, they were thin and had a multitude of lacerations to their faces. Felix had a black eye, Cassius a cut lip, and Titus had lost a part of his left ear.

Only when they had finished eating and were settled by the fire did Odell ask them to talk about their journey.

"It's so good to have you back, but by the look of you, you've been through an awful time of it." Observed Odell.

"It's good to be back, but to be honest, there were times when I believed I would never see you or the settlement again," said Felix, Titus and Cassius nodded vigorously. Felix continued, "I am a tough soldier, from a family of tough soldiers, but this was one of the hardest journeys of my life. Our trip back to Italia with Flavia was straightforward, we were lucky we did not encounter storms or vagabonds. When we reached Maximus's estate, we were treated as heroes by his father and the rest of the family, until two things combined to make us outcasts. First, word reached Maximus senior that his son had produced an heir with a woman in Britannia," despite herself, Odell blushed, "Flavia was hauled in front of the family and interrogated, but she refused to say whether she had heard the rumour or indeed knew of such a child. Second, a couple days after Flavia's grilling, in the dead of night, she fled with her lover the ex-gladiator Spiculus."

"Sorry did you say Spiculus?" Asked Marcus, getting to his feet, Felix nodded. "I fought with him in Rome, he is a brave and kind man. Pray continue Felix."

"As a parting shot to her dead husband's family, Flavia left a note in it she claimed to have a legal document which transferred Maximus's estate to her prior to his death, this sent Maximus senior into apoplexy, he ranted and raved for days about the law not allowing for such a transaction. But the truth is, things are changing in the Republic and prominent women are beginning to have rights to land and property. Anyway, in his anger, he turned on us, his son's friends, and accused us of being complicit in Flavia's treachery. Of course, we strenuously denied it, but nevertheless, he had us detained and tied up in the stables. Luckily, some of the servants were sympathetic, they had loved Maximus deeply and were sure he would not have wanted this for us. So, under the cover of darkness, they released us, gave us horses, and sent us on our way. We rode like the wind until we were forced to rest the horses. On our second full day, we took a wrong turn and found ourselves pursued by a gang of Germanic mercenaries. Of course, we had to fight our way out, which was not helped by the arrival of soldiers sent by Maximus's father. Weirdly, however, we ended up fighting together against the Germanic rebels, and, unexpectedly, the survivors did not stop us from leaving."

"My goodness, it's quite an ordeal you describe," said Odell, frowning.

"There is more, I'm afraid," said Felix.

"Well, pray, don't let me stop you."

"On the boat back across the water to Britannia, a mighty storm struck but, during a lull there was time to make repairs to our kit, one morning, I took my left shoe off to re-sew the seam when something caught my eye. The edge of a piece of parchment was just peeping out of the sole, someone had sewn it in there, I unpicked the stitches and pulled gently, but had to call Cassius across to make sense of if, for I do not read. Cassius will tell you what it said."

"It was a legal document outlining the transfer of Maximus Augustus's entire vineyard and estate to Flavia Augustus, signed by a magistrate and five witnesses and dated a month before Maximus died."

"I don't understand. Why would Flavia put it in your shoe?" Asked Marcus.

"I think she knew she could never take advantage of it, but wanted to keep it safe for Tamm," said Odell.

"That makes the stakes extremely high. I cannot see Maximus's father letting this go. I think we should expect a visit from him," said Marcus, frowning.

"Then we will make sure we are ready, but no matter what happens, Tamm stays with us. In the future, if he wishes to take up his inheritance, he can decide to do so. We must ensure he does not lose the opportunity to do so."

"I completely agree with you."

It was as Marcus had predicted. Two months later, word reached the settlement a prominent Roman with a small army had landed at the port at the head of the river and was asking about the son of a Britannia woman and Roman Soldier. Odell had already decided it would be best to take the fight to Maximus senior, to keep Tamm out of harm's way, she had given much thought to the options open to her; she knew it was impossible to predict how this entitled Roman would react.

Having established from several spies Maximus's army comprised of fifty well-armed private soldiers, Odell decided to ambush them in a dense area of the forest, a couple of days' walk from the settlement. So, she had them followed from the port to the chosen location, but on the afternoon of the first day, word reached her to force a change of plan. A group of well-armed marauders had ambushed Maximus senior and his men. Odell mobilised her men and, with Marcus at her side, they made their way at speed towards the fray. As they arrived, it was obvious the fight was going badly for the senior Roman and his men. They were met with a scene of carnage and in that moment, Odell realised she had a choice. Stand back and allow the raiders to wipe out the romans thus ending any risk to Tamm, or fight alongside him and defeat the murdering looters. As if he sensed her mind, Marcus took her hand, and they ran forward into the chaos.

Although in his late forties, Maximus senior fought with energy, but it did not take Odell long to realise his men were not up to the task, she ran forward rapidly, shooting off arrows. So transfixed by Odell was Maximus senior he did not see the butt of a sword swing towards his head. With the felling of their leader, many of his men lost their nerve and fled.

It took a couple of hours for Odell and her men to dispatch the robbers, and a couple more to assess the injured Romans for their journey back to the settlement, carts had to be sent for to carry the injured.

Twenty Romans survived and were taken to the settlement, to the long hut where their wounds received treatment, included in that number was Maximus's unconscious father.

At dusk, Odell entered the long hut to check on the men, she had yet to decide if they were to be prisoners or guests, much would depend on Maximus senior, who was now conscious.

"I wondered when I might see you again, I owe you a great debt, you saved my life and that of many of my men, I am truly grateful and somewhat at a loss as to why you helped us when you must have known the purpose of my visit?"

"You are welcome, I am not in the habit of standing by and watching a massacre occur, even if I don't see eye to eye with those fighting."

"I now understand what my son saw in you, you possess a presence, a beauty, and you are brave, you sprang into the action like a gazelle leaping through the forest, you are a force of nature."

"As pleasant as your compliments are, I'm afraid they will not change my mind, so, let's get to the crux of why you are here, my son Tamm, I will say this once only, he stays here with us." Odell looked directly into Maximus's eyes.

"Had you said that to me a few days ago, I would have laughed in your face and suggested you were clearly unaware of who you were dealing with, I might even have insulted you by suggesting you are nothing but an uneducated native, but that is clearly not the case and regrettably for me, my fortunes have changed. May I ask you a question about your relationship with my son?"

"You may ask, but I may decline to answer."

"Fair enough, did you know he was married when you joined with him?"

"I did not."

"Over the last day I've had time to reflect on my behaviour, on my values and I wonder if the grief I feel, clouded my judgement, I was intent on revenge at any cost and I'm not proud of how I treated people especially Flavia. I see now it would be wrong to take your son, it's not something I wish to do, even if I could, I ask just one small favour, however, may I be permitted to meet him?"

"Odell stood before Maximus, hands on her hips, she took a deep breath, before turning to Freya who was at her side.

"Please fetch Marcus and Tamm," then she turned to Maximus.

"Do not frighten Tamm, he is strong, but also a sweet natured, shy eight-year-old."

Maximus nodded.

Marcus and Tamm entered the barn, Tamm on the gladiator's shoulders, they were laughing about something as they entered. Conversations in the long hut immediately ceased, all eyes were on Tamm, Maximus senior struggled to his feet.

"Hello Tamm, it's good to meet you, my name is Maximus Augustus, my son, was your father." Marcus helped Tamm down from his shoulders and encouraged him forward with a smile and a little shove, Maximus and Marcus exchanged glances.

Tamm bowed, before fixing Maximus with a quizzical gaze.

"Tamm you have the same eyes as your father, I am sad that you did not get to meet him, but I am honoured to make your acquaintance, I am indebted to your mother for my life, I hope that soon I will be permitted to return to my country and that perhaps one day when you are older you might visit."

"Thank you, my mother is a wise and great leader, I am sure she will be kind. One day, I'd like to visit, I'm sorry you lost your son, my father, but I feel lucky to have the protection and love of his best friend, Marcus." Bowing again, Tamm ran across to Odell for a hug before joining the other children at the far end of the barn.

Odell watched as Maximus wiped a tear from his cheek, she walked across. "I'm sorry if Tamm made you sad, he speaks from the heart."

"No, he is a special boy, I weep because I cannot believe I was intent on tearing apart your family, there has been enough sorrow to last a lifetime, Marcus, thank you for looking after Odell and Tamm."

"It is the greatest honour of my life; I love them both immeasurably."

"I can see that; I wish you all much happiness and peace."

Two weeks later Odell watched as Maximus and his men left the settlement at the start of their journey back home, as they finally disappeared into the distance a wave of relief flooded over her. Glancing across to her left she saw her beloved son play fighting with her beloved Gladiator, a huge smile spread across her face.

Twenty years later 433 AD:

It was one of those rare early summer mornings, a gentle breeze, and hazy sunlight, which hinted at the promise of greater warmth to come. Odell was busy sweeping out the chicken shed, a job she'd carried out weekly for as long as she could remember, pausing for a moment, she stood up, her back stiff with age. She wondered how her body had come to this decrepit state, she sighed, as she did so, she thought of Marcus. Seized with a sense of foreboding and fear, she instinctively knew something was wrong, and she must find him. Dropping her broom, she scurried out of the shed in the direction of the vegetable garden, age prevented a speedy approach, reaching the gate out of breath, she stopped to catch a mouthful of air as she scanned the neat vegetable beds for her love.

At the far end of the garden stood a shady oak tree, it was there that Odell caught sight of Marcus sitting on the ground with his back supported by the trunk. He was still a large, strong looking man, but she noticed his head was bowed, she ran across as fast as her arthritic body would allow, crying out his name. As she reached him, slowly, very slowly Marcus raised his head, it seemed to sap all his strength to do so, a weak smile spread across his drawn grey features, Odell dropped to her knees in front of him placing her hands either side of his face searching his large brown, beautiful eyes.

"Please, no, no, no," she shouted.

"My love, we knew this time would come, we talked about it, I'm older than you, it was always likely I'd be the first to go." His voice a mere whisper.

"Please, no, no," Odell's whole body shook.

"I'm ready my love."

"But I'm not ready," sobbed Odell.

"My darling, I'll always be with you, you are the love of my life and while I wish I could stay, my body is broken, I'm tired, I need to sleep now. We will be together again in the afterlife; I do not fear death."

"I'll go get help; we'll soon fix you up."

"No, it's my time, come and listen to my chest, my life blood is slipping away." Odell pressed her ear to Marcus's chest, the boom of his heart was audible, but it was slow and erratic.

"I will always be by your side, if there is a perfect time to go this is it, in your arms in the place we built our life together, a life filled with such joy."

"I love you, Marcus."

"I love you Odell, my warrior queen."

Marcus's eyes closed as he took his last breath, Odell clung to him, tears flowing in tracks down her dusty cheeks, she kissed his lips one last time. Not knowing how to go on without him, her whole body ached with loss. She was brought back to reality by a sharp stabbing pain in her chest, she cried out. It was so agonising; it felt as if it would split her in half, as she struggled to take a breath, the merest hint of a smile appeared on her blue lips for she realised, after all she would be able to lie in Marcus's arms forever. A calmness flooded over her, she closed her eyes, and as she slipped away, she marvelled at the privilege of true love, so often searched for, so seldom found. Her last image, the first time she locked eyes with Marcus, a lifetime ago.

As the years passed, often, there were sightings of a large black man in the company of a female archer, bow raised, running through the forest laughing, in pursuit of fallow deer, to this day the sightings persist.

Present Day:

Harriet's sleep had been fitful, the shocking revelations of the violence inflicted on Ada by Philip Russell had angered and upset her deeply. She now wondered if she should speak to Ada about it, or leave the matter be, the problem was she wasn't very good at keeping secrets, she didn't like secrets. Then her thoughts turned to Henry, handsome Henry, lovely Henry, why had she not heard from him? Hopefully he was okay? Perhaps there wasn't a signal where he was? Disturbed by her mobile vibrating, she picked it up to see it was Mike calling her, it was 0545hrs.

"Harriet, you need to get to Police HQ. There's been another death. Harriet didn't answer. She was too busy trying to take in Mike's words. "Did you hear me? Are you there?"

"Yes, I'm here. Oh my God, who?"

"Sharon Jones."

"Fuck, Mike, what happened?"

"Officers were called to a disturbance at her house just after midnight."

"And?"

"First impressions were a struggle occurred during which Sharon received fatal injuries. Her husband is still with us, but in intensive care, he also has head injuries. At first, officers thought it was a domestic incident, but Paul Jones and Steven Leach think not."

"Give me half an hour and I'll meet you in the incident room."

"No problem."

Harriet arrived as Derek Wynn was busy issuing instructions. The room was frenetic, officers rushing back and forth. As Harriet walked in, Derek looked up and gestured for her to join him.

"Boss, I'm so sorry, I didn't see this coming and should have. Bloody should have engaged my brain. I've let you down."

"Stop it, you know as well as I do, this is not your fault, it's no one's fault."

"But…"

"But nothing, our focus has been Fairview and rightly so, if you think about it logically, there was no sign Sharon Jones was in danger, all we had was a phone conversation overheard by Ethel which appeared to her to be an argument between Sharon and another person unknown. It's all very tenuous, and it's hearsay. If it will put your mind at rest, have another conversation with

Ethel to see if you can get any further information, but I think it's unlikely to bear fruit."

"Thank you, boss."

"You are most welcome. Now, have you heard from Henry recently?"

"No, I need to speak to Kate and see if she's had contact."

"Good idea, and please stop beating yourself up." Harriet managed a smile and went in search of Kate Squires.

Kate was in a side room, staring at a computer screen, she only looked up when Harriet walked in. Smiling widely, she beckoned Harriet across.

"Hi there, good timing on your part. I think I may have found something to help us.

Harriet grabbed a chair and placed it next to Kate's.

"This is Alice Goodman's work computer. I think she may have been out of her depth. Rarely have I seen such a disorganised set of files. She was no record keeper, that's for sure, but I found a file containing photos and pen pictures of all the medical staff working at Fairview."

"And?"

"And look at this image of nurse Daniel Croft. Whilst he bears very little resemblance to Joe Wilson, there are a couple of things that make me think it is the same man. When we went for drink, I noticed two things about him first, he has unusually green eyes, more blue than green, and yet not blue, if that makes sense?" Harriet nodded, "he also has mismatched ear lobes, one is narrow, the other large and flat, now, whilst Daniel Croft's face looks nothing like the Joe Wilson I remember, if I enlarge the photo, look at the eyes and the earlobes."

"Oh, my goodness, yes, I think you may have something, are you thinking he's had surgery?"

"I'd say so, what is also interesting is I could not verify his nursing qualifications."

"I'd hazard a guess, that's because he doesn't have any, this is excellent work, Kate, we need to let Derek Wynn know immediately, now, at least we know who we are looking for."

"Yes, I agree, but I also think we should make sure Alice Goodman is protected even though she's in custody, he's a clever man and may try to get to her, we need to find out what she knows and how Daniel came to be employed at Fairview."

"You are right, also, can I suggest you speak to Derek in confidence, we don't want it to leak out that we can identify Joe Wilson," Kate nodded.

As they walked to the incident room together, Mike Taylor arrived.

"Harriet, the boss wants us to go to the crime scene immediately."

"Okay, sorry Kate, please update Derek and I'll catch up with you later, oh, have you by any chance heard from your dad in the last 24hrs?"

"No problem, and no, but he did say he might be out of contact for a few days, why have you?"

"No."

"I'm sure he's fine, I'll try to make contact later."

Sharon and Malcolm Jones lived in a three-bedroomed house in the grounds of St Johns Primary School on the edge of town. The house was unremarkable on the outside, but as Harriet and Mike entered, the way it had been styled struck Harriet. They followed the taped off route, the hallway had expensive wood flooring, a grand oak staircase, and light oak internal doors. They made their way into the lounge through a door on the left, it was a large L shaped room, expensive sofas and furnishings, a huge flat screen television, an elaborate mantlepiece, a huge rectangular silver mirror the length of one side of the room and black and white artwork on the walls and side tables. Mostly, they were professional portraits of Sharon and Malcolm, as Harriet examined a photo, Paul Jones walked in carrying an armful of personal protective equipment.

"Hello, you two, Scene suits, overshoes, and gloves for you, the key scene is upstairs, but I want to show you where I think the attacker entered.

We are still very much in the process of gathering evidence, although the lounge has been processed and discounted. So, once you've put this lot on, come, and find me."

"Mike, I feel so bad, I should have anticipated this."

"Nonsense, Derek said you blame yourself, it's not your fault, none of us could have predicted this."

"Couldn't we?"

"No, now, stop this. you are still the brilliant detective we all know and love," Mike winked at Harriet, who broke into a grin.

"Thanks Mike, now let's go and see if we can help Paul and Steven."

They found Paul in a large ornate kitchen, a mass of stainless steel and marbled tops.

"Now, let me run you through how I think the offender entered the property, you see the backdoor mechanism? It has not been tampered with, but step outside and look under this flowerpot and there's a spare key. All the offender had to do was look through a hole in the fence in the back alley, to discover the key's location. I'm told by a neighbour Malcolm always enters the house via the back door. When we arrived at the scene, it was possible to see footprints in the dew leading to the back fence, there are scuff marks on it, and traces of blood on the wood, we have carefully removed this for analysis. The alley at the back is sufficiently wide to allow a car to pass, fresh tyre marks are visible, I have taken casts for further investigation." Neither Harriet nor Mike made comment, but both took notes before following Paul back into the kitchen and through a door into the hallway.

"Now, the main scene is upstairs in the master bedroom, Sharon is still in situ, but an air ambulance took Malcolm to St. James's hospital to their specialist head injury unit. Sadly, he has suffered life changing wounds. It's not clear when or even if he will be able to speak to us, when he was checked in at the hospital, however, one of our sharp-eyed officers spotted a watch on his wrist, not just any watch but, a rare a vintage 1974 Rolex Submariner."

"Major George Moore's watch," said Harriet.

"Indeed, it would seem so."

They reached the doorway to the main bedroom, both Harriet and Mike had seen many gruesome crime scenes over the years, but this one made them gasp, Steven Leach came forward to greet them.

"Hello, you two, first impressions please? Derek is keen to know your initial gut reaction to this," Steven was looking directly at both detectives.

"Blind Fury," said Harriet.

"Blind rage," said Mike, as he stepped further into the room.

"You are looking at a furious confrontation, ferocious violence, an utter loss of control," Steven continued, "you can see Sharon suffered massive trauma to the back of the head, she is lying face down on the carpet in a pool of blood, note her arms over her head, presumably to shield her from the blows. We have yet to find the item used to cave in her skull, as you can see, it left us with a compromised scene because of the volume of blood present. It's made the spatter stain patterns unrecognisable on the floor. But we are left with the blood droplet pattern from the weapon as it was swung backwards and forwards."

"Where was Malcolm found?" Asked Mike.

"On the floor of the ensuite, it looks like he crawled in there, he managed to lock the door before losing consciousness, he had his mobile in his bloodied hand, but it doesn't look like he was able summon help before he passed out." Said Paul Jones.

"How did it come to be reported?" Asked Harriet.

"It seems three or four local youths were how should I put it, exploring the school grounds when they heard sustained screaming coming from the caretaker's house. They are being interviewed as we speak, hopefully further details will come to light."

"What I can't get over is the way someone has ripped apart the room." Mike moved towards a built-in wardrobe, the doors were hanging off their hinges, someone had smashed them with something heavy, like a sledgehammer. Their contents thrown across the floor, some had been ripped into pieces, shoe boxes and other boxes lay shredded on the floor. Sharon's dressing table drawers lay smashed on the once white carpet, their contents strewn over the floor, and the bed, had been slashed and torn into tatters.

"It's disturbing, no that doesn't even get close to describing it, its gruesome," Harriet pulled a face.

Harriet and Mike left the bedroom and went outside for a chat.

"My God, Mike, do we really think this could be the work of Joe Wilson? If we do, then he is far more unstable than even I thought. It's a terrifying thought, to be honest."

"I don't think we really know Joe Wilson; we've uncovered brief glimpses of the man. If you remember, we found Florence Ballard in a grave behind the milking parlour at Rock Farm, she had suffered blunt force trauma to the head, only with Sharon, it went way beyond smashing her over the head. Joe only came into the frame for Florence's death when we realised her death occurred after his brother David had committed suicide and therefore could not be the perpetrator, the next time Joe surfaced was when you recognised him from a photo and intervened in his date with Kate Squires, but unfortunately, he eluded us and disappeared. Who knows what he's capable of, but I think we need to concentrate on finding him."

"I totally agree. Kate has made progress; she thinks she's identified him from staff photos at Fairview. We believe we know what he looks like now. It seems obvious he's had facial surgery, but I asked her to tell no-one other than Derek to prevent any leaks."

"That is good news."

"Guys, could you come upstairs again, please?" Paul Jones's head appeared at an open upstairs window.

"I'm not sure how to broach this, but as we turned Sharon over, I noticed something in her mouth; inside a tiny plastic bag I found a note addressed to you, Harriet," said a white-faced Steven Leach.

Harriet's mouth dropped open as her knees went weak, she grabbed the door frame and took a deep breath.

"What does it say, Paul?"

"*Oh, Detective Lacey, Detective Lacey, I'm disappointed in you. I thought you might be a worthy adversary, but it seems you are not paying attention, or maybe you don't possess the intellect to keep up.*"

"What a shit," Mike put his arm around Harriet's before continuing, "do not take this to heart, do not, he is trying to rile you, to force a confrontation, stay calm."

"I totally agree. Just because he's thrown down the gauntlet doesn't mean you should take up the fight," said a frowning Paul Jones.

"I'm okay, don't worry. I promise I won't do anything foolish or impulsive."

That evening, Harriet could not settle, Amelia had gone to stay with her father's parents for a couple of days, and usually Harriet enjoyed the peace using the time to catch up with chores or with friends, or both, but tonight she felt out of sorts for two reason, Joe Wilson had got to her, and, although she had promised Mike she would not do anything rash, a deep seated anger was growing within. She was determined to put an end to his murdering spree. But before she could concentrate on work, she needed to contact Henry, satisfy herself he was safe and well. Never had someone had such a profound effect on her, and she refused to lose him, he was always on her mind, sometimes in the background, but always there, she longed for his touch, for his scent, for his mouth on hers. The doorbell rang. Harriet put on her slippers and made her way from the sofa to the front door, to see it was Henry's daughter Kate.

"Come in, come in."

"Thank you, I thought it would be easier to come and chat in person."

"Is everything alright, you look flushed?"

"Harriet, I can't get hold of Dad, and whilst I keep telling myself he is bound to be fine; I'm concerned now, have you heard from him?" Harriet shook her head.

"I'm just waiting for a call back from Cyrus, he has contacts in Yemen, he has contacts all over the world," said Kate, smiling despite herself.

"I haven't seen Cyrus for ages, how is he? I do so love his company," said Harriet, pouring them both a glass of red wine.

"He's fine, never seems to age, he's looked in his early seventies ever since I can remember, busy as always with his antiques and, of course, his work with the Guardians."

"Yes, of course," several years before, Harriet had come to learn about the Guardians, it seemed a distant world now, as her hand instinctively touched the precious gold, sapphire mounted pendant around her neck.

Kate's mobile burst into life, she moved about the room, talking animatedly to someone, after about five minutes, the call ended.

"Is he missing?" Harriet placed her hand on Kate's.

"Yes, it seems last week he left Saada in the north-western highlands for Taiz in southwest Yemen, it's a journey of nearly 500 km."

"But?" Harriet could feel her lower lip quivering.

"But the group he was travelling with has disappeared, Médecins San Frontières have mobilised and sent a group of experienced guides to find them, I'm told it's too early to panic, maybe they have broken down or must travel on foot through the Yemeni Highlands."

"Is there anything we can do?" Harriet wiped a tear from her face.

"No, not yet, Cyrus is all over it, I trust him, he's going to speak to all his contacts in the country and get back to me, I was told to tell you not to worry. He is confident that Dad is alive and well."

"I wish I had his confidence."

"I suggest, we let Cyrus do his thing, but if there is no news in the next day or so, perhaps we will have to think about how we might be able to help? What do you think?"

"I think that's very sensible, we should try to be patient and let the experts on the ground do their jobs."

"Agreed."

"But you should know, I'll do anything in my power to find your dad, I love him so much I can't bear to think of a life without him," Harriet's shoulders began to shake, Kate wrapped her arms around her, and the two women hugged.

CHAPTER 20

Present Day:

Ada lay in bed, mulling over whether she could be bothered to get up or not. Once again, she found herself overwhelmed by a low mood, how many times in her life had she felt like this she wondered? Too many to recall. It had started the morning after her husband Philip first laid hands on her, many years before, and try as she might, she could not banish it, why? Maybe because she had never allowed herself to confront the pain.

A couple of hours later, Linda, Ada's carer, persuaded her to move from the bed to a chair by the window, as she watched a robin serenade her, there was a loud knock at the door, she turned to see a familiar face; a smile spread across Ada's lined face.

"Why, if it isn't the lovely Mr Taylor!"

"Morning Ada, may I come in?" Ada nodded. "A little bird tells me you are in the doldrums."

"That would be Linda, no doubt."

"Well, I couldn't possibly reveal my source, now, could I?"

"No, I suppose not. Have you had breakfast yet?"

"Actually no, I missed it this morning, are you inviting me on a date, Ada?"

"Of course! Please join me, I'll text Linda and let her know."

Fifteen minutes later, Ada and Mike were tucking into porridge and toast, coffee, and orange juice.

"Ada, I don't wish to pry, but what's brought on this change in you?" asked Mike, taking her hand.

"Oh, don't worry about me, I get like this often, I'll get over it, it's part of life, it most likely keeps happening because I refuse to face up to my past."

"Well, that's not an easy thing to do for anyone."

"No, I've been determined not to let what happened to me define me, but it has literally stayed with me all these years and, at times, blighted my life."

"Then maybe now is a good time to exorcise your demons?"

"Maybe."

"I actually wanted to talk to you about your past," Ada sat upright and locked eyes with Mike, "the account you gave Harriet of your life with Philip affected her deeply. Moved by how isolated and alone you were, she wanted to see if it was possible to corroborate what you told her. She has a deep respect for you and wanted to see if it was possible to prove your account.

What she did not want to do was to add to your pain, after she asked me to investigate, we spoke, both concerned that maybe we should have asked your permission first, that you might see us as meddling in your affairs, that you might be angry? By the way, Harriet does not know I've come to talk to you."

"I'm listening, young man. What did you find?"

"I warn you, some of it is upsetting. Hard to repeat."

"Just tell me, Mike, warts and all."

Mike talked Ada through his findings, it took longer than he had expected, for she interrupted frequently. Ada smiled and clapped her hands together as he told her of David Bryant's account of the first time she complained to the police, his recall of her injuries, and his regret at remaining quiet when threatened by Philip. The smile widened when Mike read Greg Myles' pocketbook entry to her.

"All these years I thought no one believed me, no one cared what happened to me, but that wasn't the case. All these years I've had a deep-seated sense of injustice. The grief of isolation overwhelmed me, and yet it seems all the time there were those who believed and tried to help. Mike, have you any idea what a difference this makes to me? It changes everything."

"There is a little more to tell you, Philip Russell was the subject of many complaints over the years made both by officers and members of the public, complaints that were all marked up as unsubstantiated. The Constabulary has reactivated all these, and they are currently investigating them. Unfortunately, Sergeant Bell died a few years ago, but there are other officers alive and happy to talk. The current Chief Constable would like to meet you if you agree, to apologise at the way the constabulary fell way below the standard expected. In addition, David Bryant and Greg Myles would dearly like to meet you."

"I would like that very much indeed. Thank you, Mike."

"You are most welcome, Ada. You are an inspirational survivor."

Ada got up from her chair and gave Mike a long, hard hug.

"I don't know about you, but I need a large glass of sherry," Ada helped herself.

"Not for me, thank you. I'm on duty. There was a time when I wouldn't have given a second thought to drinking on duty, but I'm a changed man!"

Ada laughed, "now, let's talk about Harriet. I hear her beau has gone missing in Yemen. I know her well enough to guess that she might do something rash like going in search of him, am I right?"

"You are, but she's torn between her duty to our current case and her feelings for Henry. Harriet is one of the most instinctive and clever detectives I've ever worked with, an extraordinary officer. She is also one of the most committed and will not rest until we apprehend the prime suspect, especially as he's now made it personal."

"Oh Really?"

"Yes, I probably shouldn't tell you, but I trust you. He left a note for her with the last victim."

"What a scoundrel."

"Indeed, I think we are moving in on the rogue, it's only a matter of time before we catch him and then Harriet will be free to go in search of Henry. I just pray he's not in too much of a fix. Anyway, I've already had a conversation with our boss Derek Wynn about taking unpaid leave to travel to Yemen with Harriet, that way, at least I can keep an eye on her."

"That sounds like a fine idea, Mike, doesn't she have a daughter at home?"

"She has a son and a daughter, her son is at university, and I've already spoken to Henry's daughter Kate Squires to ask her if she'd be prepared to step in to help look after Amelia, they get on extremely well. Harriet's mother Jane has also offered to help."

"It sounds like you have it all sorted, now all that needs to happen is for this case to end."

That afternoon, word reached Ada Harriet was in the building, she sent an invitation for tea and cake.

"Good afternoon, Ada, how are you today?" asked a smiling Harriet as she joined her at her round walnut table.

"Well, I'm remarkably improved from early this morning, Mike came to see me and told me all about his investigation in South Gloucestershire. Don't look taken aback, it's fine, for the first time in many years, I feel free of my past, thank you both for what you've done. It's completely changed my perspective on life. "

"You are most welcome Ada, good old Mike, I didn't know how to broach it with you, I thought you might be angry with me for meddling."

"Not at all, I feel vindicated, I do however, have one question for you, if that's okay?

"Of course, fire away."

"I got the distinct feeling Mike left something out, didn't tell me everything, perhaps, to spare my feelings?"

"Oh? What sort of thing?"

"Did he by any chance come across any medical records?"

Harriet gasped despite herself, she was aware of a heavy feeling in her stomach, she wondered how she should reply, playing for time, she nodded.

"I thought as much, I could see it in his eyes, he was conflicted, so, you know about my miscarriage then?"

"Yes, I'm so, so, sorry Ada, the last thing either of us wanted was to churn up the hurt of the past, I should have known better."

"Don't, please don't." Ada held up a hand, Harriet felt helpless, what could she possibly say to make this better?

"For many years I refused to think about it, pushed it from my mind, told myself it had not happened. Later, no matter how hard I tried, it would creep into my thoughts, my feelings were complicated, on the one hand, I was relieved I was no longer carrying that despicable brute's offspring. On the other, it broke my heart to lose my unborn son. As the years rolled by, I also had to come to terms with the realisation there would be no further opportunity to have children, but I am far from alone in this experience, and I take some comfort from knowing that my work helped many women, and some men caught up in the cycle of abuse. I helped them to break free and I feel privileged to have been able to do so."

Harriet put her arms around her friend. "Ada, you are truly inspirational, one of the most fascinating and able women I have ever met."

"Thank you dear, that means a great deal to me, I now feel I have faced my past, made sense of it, and survived, I feel uplifted, as if an enormous weight has gone. Anyway, enough about me, how are you doing?"

"That's kind of you to ask, I'm okay, worried about Henry obviously, and trying to find a breakthrough in this case, I'm not sure I'm exactly on top of my game."

"I'm sure everything will work out just fine, you just need to believe in yourself, I have it on good authority you are considered an extraordinary detective. Instead of doubting yourself, do what you do best and catch the bastard."

"Well put like that, I can't very well do anything else! Thank you for giving me the kick up the backside I needed."

"You are most welcome, dear, now, before you solve this, I want to show you something I have rarely shared." Harriet leaned in as Ada produced a large wooden box from underneath the table, she removed the lid and took out a folded piece of paper.

"My mother gave me this box when I reached eighteen with this handwritten note, it simply says: *"This is your heritage, guard it carefully."* Well, I've kept it all these years, with no children to pass it onto, I think I'd like to find out a bit more, if that's even possible."

"How intriguing, I know someone who would be delighted to help you; his name is Cyrus Hart; he is a dear friend. He deals in antiques but is also incredibly knowledgeable and a lovely man to boot."

"He sounds perfect." And with that Ada reached into the box and took out something wrapped in tissue paper. Carefully, she unwrapped it; out of the paper Harriet saw a fragile-looking choker, a black leather string from which a large tooth hung from a silver clasp.

"It's beautiful; is it a lion's tooth, perhaps?"

"I think it maybe, but I do not know how old it is or what its significance is."

Next Ada removed a brooch from a red velvet bag. "You can tell this is extremely old too, it is intricate, and I believe it's gold, look at the workmanship." Harriet stared at the golden circle inlaid with swirls and spirals; "it's exquisite Ada."

"I'm no expert, but I think it may have been used to hold a cloak together. This is of such high quality, I think it may have belonged to someone of high standing. Now, the next item is a signet ring, and I'm pretty sure it's roman, look, I'm only guessing, but I think it's a man's ring, it appears to be gold with some sort of orange stone at its centre into which a leaf has been carved."

"Ada, it's amazing; I feel incredibly honoured to see these treasures."
Ada took out the next item, it was clearly heavy. For she had to use both hands. Carefully she unwrapped it from a piece of red velvet to reveal a bronze eagle, maybe ten inches by six, it was difficult to say. Also, with it was a piece of red and gold fabric, extremely degraded and fragile, full of holes. Harriet could just make out some partial lettering 'IX Hispania' in faded gold thread. "Ada, what is this do you think?"

"I think it may have been a Roman Legion Eagle, I've done some research. Every legion had a standard, a wooden pole topped with an eagle and a banner with the legion's name on it, to denote who they were. I hesitate to say this, but it's possible this is what's left of the standard of the Ninth Legion."

"What? The missing legion?" Whispered a wide-eyed Harriet.

"Sounds crazy, doesn't it?" Both women burst out laughing.

"There is one last item," Ada unwrapped a delicate sheet of paper from several layers of tissue paper.

"What is it, Ada?" Asked Harriet, scrutinising it.

"Some sort of document; look here, you can see writing and what looks like signatures, but I think it's written in Latin, which I do not profess to understand."

"Wow, these items are so special, it must be possible to find out more about them."

"I'm sure it is, and now is the time to do so."

"Incredible, just incredible."

"So now you've seen my heritage, whatever that means," Ada chuckled, "I have a strong feeling these items were treasured, and I want to find out more without betraying anyone or losing control of them."

"Oh Ada, this is so interesting, so exciting. Do you know anything else about your family's past? I'm told even the smallest detail can lead to new information."

"When I was first given custody of them by my mother, I of course grilled her, she seemed to find my intense interest quite amusing, I'm not sure why, maybe they held no interest for her, but for me, the contents of this box are a thing of awe."

"So, was she able to tell you anything more?"

"Yes, a little. There is a family story passed down over the generations about a woman who lived in the Forest of Dean in Gloucestershire in a hill fort near Soudley. She was apparently involved in a love triangle between a rich Roman soldier and an Abyssinian Gladiator. It's said she bore the Roman a child before choosing the Gladiator, incredible and far-fetched, don't you think?"

"I think it's truly intriguing, the thought that you might be related to the original owners of these items sends shivers down my spine. Wouldn't it be amazing if it were possible to find out more? Cyrus is your man; incredibly well connected and he will know exactly where to look."

"Then I look forward immensely to meeting him."

"I will set it up, but a word of warning, in the meantime, keep the box and its contents safe and I'd avoid mentioning it to anyone until we have apprehended our outstanding offender. I don't want to frighten you, but he is extremely dangerous."

"Good point, don't worry about me, I do not frighten easily."

"I know you don't, but I will confess even I am a little fearful of what he might do."

"Well, let's hope your plan works." Harriet had to look in Ada's eyes to confirm she was being playful, but was she? Harriet clutched her stomach and tried not to think of the consequences should she fail.

Present Day:

Harriet went in search of Ethel. She found her in her room, knitting.

"Morning, Ethel. What in heaven's name are you doing?"

"I'm taking part in Ada's knitting competition; there's a bottle of sherry for the longest scarf and I plan to win it!"

"Of course there is! Good for you," said Harriet, smiling, "while you knit, do you mind if I ask you a few questions?"

"Go ahead."

"You remember you told me you overheard Sharon Jones arguing with someone on the phone? Do you, by any chance, recall further detail?"

"Let me think," Ethel bit her lower lip, "I remember talk of a watch, Sharon said she was keeping it, I also remember she called the person on the line a sneaky, thieving, bastard, but there's nothing else that comes to mind, unless it's important it was Mothering Sunday?"

"That's great, thank you, Ethel, good luck with the competition."

As Harriet walked into Fairview's carpark, she made a call "Steven, it's Harriet, did you by any chance, find Sharon Jones's mobile?"

"Yes, it was on the floor under her body, Kate is interrogating it as we speak."

"Brilliant, thank you, I'll pop in and see her."

A short time later, Harriet found Kate in her office. "Harriet, it's good to see you for two reasons," said a smiling Kate.

"Oh Yes?"

"Yes, I've literally just put the phone down, Cyrus has news regarding Dad, it's not as definitive as I'd have liked, but I'm feeling a bit more optimistic, he's apparently been spotted with a group of men in the mountains between Saada and Taiz, so we know he's alive. But details are sketchy as to whether he's there voluntarily or not, Cyrus hopes to have more specific information later."

"It's something though, thank goodness he's alive, I wish there was something I could do to help."

"Me too."

"You said there were two reasons you were pleased to see me?"

"Ah yes, I have been looking at Sharon Jones's mobile and there are some pretty cryptic texts I want to look at more closely."

"That sounds promising, are you by any chance able search for phone calls made on Mothering Sunday this year?"

"I'm sure I can, just a minute, there is one number that comes up several times that day."

"May I have it please?"

"Sure, I'll text it to you, what are you up to?"

"Just a hunch at the moment."

"Fair enough."

As Harriet walked to her car, her mobile sprang into life, she glanced at the screen, it was the number Kate had just texted, she stopped in her tracks, her mouth suddenly dry.

"Hello Harriet, well, you seem to have picked your game up a bit, I'm reasonably impressed you thought to look at Sharon's phone, but to be fair, you could have done so a day ago."

"Who is this?"

"Oh, come on, we're not going to play that game, are we?"

Harriet took a deep breath, "Joe, I haven't got time for this, now, what do you want?"

"I'm just letting you know I'm here, I'm watching you, by the way, I don't hold out much hope you will be able to detain me, you see I'm far cleverer than you give me credit for, and I'm just getting started. And don't go thinking now Fairview is locked down, I can't gain access. I very much can, and I will, well nice talking to you."

As the line went dead, Harriet felt a sense of nausea creep over her, it was all she could do to keep upright. She leant against her car for support, a few deep breaths later, she went in search of Derek Wynn.

Derek was in his office with Mike Taylor, Harriet knocked and entered.

"Whatever's the matter? You're as white as a sheet," said Derek, getting to his feet, but Mike had already found Harriet a chair.

"Now take your time and tell us what's happened," said Derek.

After Harriet had relayed her encounter with Joe Wilson, Mike broke the initial silence.

"Fuck."

"I couldn't have put it better myself," said Derek.

"I think Joe Wilson is fixated, with getting one over on the police," said Harriet.

"I completely agree. He's pitting himself against you, or rather, what you symbolise, which in my book makes him dangerous and unpredictable. For Joe Wilson, this is a game, a challenge," said Mike.

"What concerns me is this has the potential to get out of hand, I have a responsibility for your safety, I would be astounded if he isn't watching you closely, we must be extremely careful," Derek pulled his left hand through his jet-black hair.

"Well, that sociopath will not intimidate me. He is clever and won't be easy to stop."

"We stick to the plan, but Harriet, you will have to agree to additional security measures."

"Yes, boss."

A couple of nights later, Harriet woke with a start. Her mobile had burst into life. "Hello?"

"Sarge, it's DC Claire Royale; the target is in the building. I repeat in the building heading towards the nurse's station on the second floor."

Harriet rubbed her eyes; Rita Pritchard's office was pitch black. She moved to the edge of her camp bed and swung her legs over; she was now in a sitting position.

"That's unexpected. Okay, noted, send a radio message to the teams, use Channel 5. I'm on my way, stick to the plan."

"Will do."

Harriet used her mobile light to move around the room, once she's put on her shoes, she walked towards the door, gently turning the handle, she peered out, the hallway was clear, night lights provided sufficient brightness to move around, she was calm, clear about what was required, no heroics on her part. But why, she wondered, had the target chosen night-time to make his move? It didn't fit with what they knew of him.

Harriet tip-toed her way across the entrance hall to the staircase and began her ascent, keeping to the left-hand side of the stairs. She could hear her heartbeat in her ears. As she reached the first landing, she heard a creak behind her. It was too late, no time to react; something hit her on the head, then nothing, blackness, darkness.

Awaking in a pitch-black room, Harriet did not know how long she'd been unconscious. She rubbed her head; it felt sore and was tacky to the touch, a sure sign of blood. She felt slightly nauseous and disorientated, no restraints, but her mobile and radio were missing. As she came to, she realised she was cold; she could just make out a series of muffled sounds somewhere nearby. She felt around in the darkness for something she could use to attract attention.

Ada had just finished reading the last chapter of her book when she heard someone turn the door handle to her room. With remarkable quickness, she turned the bedside light out and pulled the covers over her. Only her nose and eyes were visible. She screwed her eyes tight shut and listened. The door opened and closed, a key turned in the lock, she was trapped; she strained to hear what was going on.

Someone was moving about; opening her eyes slowly, she could just make out a silhouette in their torchlight. The intruder was systematically going through her drawers, removing precious belongings; filled with a sense of outrage, she cried out.

"What the bloody hell do you think you're doing?"

Startled, the figure jumped towards the door, but instead of fleeing, turned on the main light, Ada could clearly see a man dressed in a Fairview nursing uniform.

"Why aren't you asleep, Ada?" Hissed the intruder.

"How do you know my name?"

"I make it a rule to know every resident, you should be asleep, it's three thirty in the morning."

"Well, I'm not."

"I have something here that will help you sleep," the man took a syringe from his pocket and walked towards her.

"You mean to make me sleep permanently."

"Oh, don't be like that Ada, it's not personal, anyway, it's not like you really need all this wealth, it's greedy."

"Joe, I'm warning you stay away from me and my things."

"How do you know my name? No, don't answer that, but know this: your friend Detective Lacey won't be coming to your rescue anytime soon, she's out of the picture, already been taken care of."

"What the hell have you done to her?"

"Well let's put it like this, she's in the dark," Joe laughed at his joke.

"But is she alright?" No reply was forthcoming, the sound of of persistent knocking on Ada's bedroom door drowned out the silence, someone was calling Ada's name.

"Stay there, I just need to deal with this," Ada watched Joe make for her door, unlock it and step outside into the corridor. Ada could hear muffled sounds, perhaps the sound of a struggle, with pounding heart, she desperately tried to come up with a plan to thwart Joe, but there was no time, he returned and re-locked the door. Ada saw he was flushed, and a little unsteady on his feet.

"What is the matter with you? You brute," shouted Ada.

"I am a man who takes what he wants, when he wants," he was laughing.

"You clearly have no shame, no concept of the emotional devastation you cause by your actions," Ada's insides were churning, her mouth dry, she'd seen enough of the less salubrious side of life to know Joe Wilson was high, and that made him dangerous.

"Look, you silly old bat, stop trying to keep me talking, stop trying to analyse me, I don't care what you think, I do my own thing, I change my plans on a whim, I was going to come here in daylight hours, but then I thought to myself it would be easier to move around the building at night for greater gains, I'm all for maximum benefit for minimum effort."

"I feel sorry for you Joe, you are clearly an extremely lonely and emotionally empty man."

"Shut the fuck up, you know nothing about me."

"Oh, on the contrary, I recognise the signs only too well, you are someone who has suffered severe emotional and physical abuse."

Joe's jaw dropped, and a heavy frown spread across his forehead, finally Ada had his attention, she'd touched a nerve, she would need to be careful, but what did she have to lose? Her situation was already precarious, so she continued to goad him.

"Oh yes, you were a child starved of love, beaten and put down by your overbearing father," from the look on Joe's face Ada could see she was on the right track, your father was a bully and no doubt a drunk."

"Fucking stop now!"

"I'm thinking he did something very bad, very bad indeed," Joe was noticeably sweating now; he covered his ears with his hands, she knew she was getting to him, but at what cost to herself?

"Did he kill someone Joe? Maybe the only person you were close to, the only person you've ever cared about, did he kill your mother?"

Without warning, Joe ran towards Ada, syringe in hand.

"Stop now! Before you do something, you will regret."

"Not in my DNA, anyway, you won't stop me, you're an ugly shrivelled, weak old lady, no match for me."

"You impudent pup, I think you'd be surprised by what I'm able to do, now stop or you will regret it."

Joe laughed loudly and continued to move forward, fearing for her life Ada did the only thing she could.

Meanwhile, Harriet had found a piece of pipe and was using it to hit the wall of her prison, it wasn't long before her arm became tired, and she had to stop. On and off for an hour, she did her best to summon help, after what seemed an eternity, she thought she heard voices, and began to shout and hit the wall once more, but still no rescue. She moved about, feeling her way around, at the far end of the room, she found a series of wall pipes and used her piece of pipe against them, she tried not to think about her plan failing, she just hoped everyone was unharmed and hoped somehow, they had captured Joe Wilson. How had he always been one step ahead? How? Unless he'd had help from within the police or Fairview? But who? Another hour passed and by now a shivering Harriet was feeling deflated, she thought about what had gone wrong, was it her fault? Or was it just that Joe Wilson was cleverer than any of them had appreciated?

It was almost 6.am when one of the search teams discovered her in an old boiler house, Mike and Derek went to see her, now in the back of an ambulance on the drive.

"Thank God you're alive," said Mike, rushing to hug her, closely followed by a visibly pale Derek Wynn.
"We were so worried about you. Are you okay?" asked Derek.

"I'm fine, just a knock to the head. I don't know if I dare ask; did we detain Joe Wilson?"

The two men exchanged glances, "yes, and no," said Derek Wynn.

"What do you mean?"

"It's complicated," said Mike before continuing, "to begin with, everything seemed to be going okay. We received the radio message Joe was in the building and made our way to the front door. It was then that things went wrong; our armed officers moved into position but discovered they could not gain entry."

"Oh God, what?" Said Harriet, feeling nauseous.

"Someone had changed the door lock codes. We lost valuable time checking the exterior of the building for a way in. In the end, we had to force entry," said Mike.

"The second problem we encountered was that all the downstairs lights were disabled, so we were literally in the dark," said Derek.

"Then, we could not contact DC Royale. She wasn't answering the radio, nor her mobile. The house was eerily silent."

"We all knew this was a risky plan. It depended on Joe Wilson coming during the day. All our profiling showed this is what he'd do, I discussed the operation at length with the Chief Constable and other senior officers, and the consensus was to evacuate the residents would not only cause distress, but seriously hamper our chances of detaining Joe without drama. As soon as I knew he was in the building, I had no choice but to order the urgent evacuation of all residents and staff. I assigned those too unwell to leave a police guard. We worked our way through the building floor by floor. I had to call for reinforcements, and this took time, when we were planning this operation, we had no intelligence Joe Wilson might have an outside source of fentanyl, we assumed he would need to go to the nurse's station for his supply, where we would be waiting to detain him." Said Derek.

"I was on the ground floor helping residents from their rooms when the whole house shook from the sound of a loud gunshot. Staff and residents were screaming and running around in circles as I ran upstairs to the third landing. I found myself outside Ada's bedroom door; I turned the door handle...," said Mike.

"And?" interrupted Harriet, with hands clasped together.

"And the door was locked." Harriet was suddenly light-headed.

"I called out for someone to find and bring a spare key. In the meantime, I tried unsuccessfully to break the door down. Approximately five long minutes passed before the spare key arrived, I feared the worse, but when I entered the room, I found Ada sitting bolt upright in bed, on the floor lay a man with a large hole in his chest, I checked, there were no signs of life."

"Ada shot him?" asked a wide-eyed Harriet.

"She did, feared for her life, Major Moore apparently insisted she have his old service revolver months before he died, 'just in case,' she hid it under her mattress."

"Is she okay?" asked Harriet.

"She seems fine, defiant, I'd say, and rightly so. She was incredibly brave; Joe still had a full syringe of what I'm guessing was fentanyl in his hand," said Mike.

"Well done, Ada, she's just such an astonishing woman," said Harriet.

"Help! Help! Send a paramedic to the third floor. Hurry, please hurry." Shouted someone from inside the house.

The paramedic treating Harriet jumped to his feet, grabbed a medical bag, and ran into the house, closely followed by Mike.

A short time later, Mike reappeared with Paramedics carrying a stretcher. The ambulance set off at speed.

"What's gone on?" asked Harriet.

"One of our officers found DC Royale unresponsive in a laundry room next to Ada's room, she was cold, clammy to the touch, her skin grey and her lips purple, she was in severe respiratory depression." Replied Mike.

"Oh my God, Fentanyl?" Said an open-mouthed Harriet.

"That's what they suspect, they administered Naloxone via a nasal device."

"What does that do?"

"I'm told that it can reverse an overdose of opioids, but it needs to be administered as soon as possible, Claire Royale's condition is touch and go."

"Bloody Joe Wilson."

"Indeed."

"Mike, can I see Ada?" asked Harriet, suddenly.

"Do you feel up to it?"

"Yes, I do."

"Very well, hold on to my arm."

They found Ada in her favourite place, the library, sitting in a wingback chair, swathed in a blanket, drinking a cup of tea, a young female officer sat next to her.

"Ah, two of my favourite people, are you okay, Harriet?"

"It's lovely to see you in such good spirits, I'm okay, just a bump to the head, are you okay? What an ordeal you went through."

"It certainly wasn't a usual evening! What a troubled soul Joe Wilson was. Did you know he was the victim of domestic abuse as a child?"

"Yes, I think we did," said Harriet. "Ada, how did you overcome him?" Harriet moved in closer.

"I'm not entirely sure, maybe a strong will to survive, and a reliance on life experience, I won't lie, it was terrifying, he seemed disconnected, shell like, any feelings he might have possessed were hidden, I just kept goading him until I got a reaction."

"You were bloody incredible," said Mike, leaning down to plant a kiss on her cheek.

"Thank you, but I was lucky, lucky George gave me his pistol, to think I objected so strongly, lucky, I knew how to use it and lucky the shot met its target, otherwise I would have been a goner."

"No not you Ada, you are a true survivor," said Harriet, stroking her hand.

"I'm interested to know how he behaved in the last few minutes of his life," said Mike.

"He sauntered towards me with a blank look on his face, I read it as indifference, I thought my heart would burst through my chest; it was beating so hard, trembling, I reached for the pistol, but I had to use both hands to hold it steady. Just for a second, an amused look flitted across his face, he leaned forward, holding the syringe above his head, ready to plunge it into me. I pulled the trigger, I was out of options, I knew he wouldn't hesitate to kill me. But can you believe it? He just rolled his eyes at me a look of complete contempt, I thought the shot had missed its target, but just as I prepared myself to die, he dropped to the floor with a loud thud, and there you have it."

"How terrifying Ada," said Harriet. Ada simply nodded.

"Is the case closed now?" She asked, looking directly at Mike.
"I think we can say the danger is over, there are a few loose ends to tie up, which include identifying and detaining Harriet's attacker and finding the whistle-blower. I suspect, Matron maybe helpful in that regard. I think she knows far more than she is saying."

"That's intriguing. I've been thinking about it, and I suspect Harriet's attacker is someone Joe leaned on or had something on. I noticed Ted Smith and Joe were often in each other's company, when everyone thought Joe was Nurse Daniel Croft." Said Ada.

"That's interesting, thank you, I'll get someone to investigate," said Harriet.

"I heard one of your officers was injured, is she going to be okay?"

"We sincerely hope so Ada, I'm just about to call the hospital for an update," said Mike.

"Ada, thank you for your help with the case, for your common sense, and for your bravery, you are truly one of the most extraordinary women I've ever had the privilege to know," said Harriet, blowing her a kiss.

"It is I who should be thanking you for your perseverance, when we first met, I was impossible and rude and …."

"Heartbroken, completely understandable," said Harriet, smiling.

"I had given up, you helped me see that all that stands between waiting to die and choosing to live is 'hope'. I do hope we can continue to be friends and from time to time you will call by for a cup of tea?"

"Of course, just you try and stop me!"

CHAPTER 22

Present Day:

Following the shooting of Joe Wilson, life got back to normal at Fairview. Ada worked tirelessly to organise a whole series of events and activities, and once more, laughter filled the building. About three weeks after Joe's death Harriet almost ran through the hallway, for she was late for tea. Breathless, she knocked on Ada's bedroom door; it swung open to reveal a beaming Cyrus.

"How lovely to see you, old girl."

"And you Cyrus, you look very handsome in that green velvet jacket," replied a breathless Harriet as she planted an enthusiastic kiss on his creased cheek.

"Harriet, we have exciting news," shouted Ada from the other side of the room, but then a loud knock cut her short as Rita Pritchard appeared in the doorway.

"Sorry to interrupt Ada, but would you mind explaining to me why there is a large swimming pool being erected on the lawn?"

"Yes, Rita, we start our summer swimming lessons tomorrow."

"Of course you do! Of course, you do! Well, thank you for clearing that up." Rita beat a hasty retreat.

Once Harriet and Cyrus had finished laughing, Ada poured the tea and cut slices of Chef Aubert's chocolate sponge, before clapping her hands in excitement.

"Guess what?"

"What?" Replied Harriet, moving her chair closer to her friend. "You remember I showed you my box of treasures? Harriet nodded. Well, Cyrus has only done the impossible, found information I could never have expected, let alone envisaged." Ada looked towards Cyrus and nodded to him.

"Well, I was extremely lucky, but I reached out to a friend who is a Roman scholar, and with his help and contacts we were able to deduce Ada's family tale of the relative involved in a love triangle with a Roman soldier and ex Gladiator, has more than a grain of truth to it."

"No!" exclaimed Harriet.

"I know! Let me tell you what we found, a record of sale from a notorious slave trader called Felix Augusta who sold a male child from Abyssinia to Quintus Agricola, the owner of the famous Ludus Magnus Gladiator Training School. Years later, there is reference to this child now as a man, fighting for Quintus. Indeed, he was his most successful gladiator, Marcus

Atilius. Next, we found reference to a campaign in 394 AD in the eastern alps close to the Frigidus river in which a Roman soldier Maximus Augustus led a cavalry charge through the enemy line to save his fellow soldiers trapped in a gully. They honoured Maximus for his bravery and at the ceremony Marcus Atilius swore his allegiance to Maximus for life. We further discovered that both men served together in the roman army in Britannia, spent some time at the Roman Fort of Corinium Dobunnorun or Cirencester, as its now known. And there's more. It seems Maximus Augustus's father was a senior political figure in Rome. He gave his son an estate in the bay of Naples, overlooking the sea, an elaborate villa, farm, and vineyard. The family crest is a vine leaf. We think the signet ring belonged to the family, but specifically to Maximus. As you may recall, the orange quartz at its centre is carved with a vine leaf."

"This is absolutely incredible, but I'm really dying to know if you found any reference to the Britannia woman at the centre of the story?" Asked Harriet, clasping her hands together.

"Well, yes, sort of, we found a legal document amongst the family's surviving archives which suggest Maximus Augustus petitioned for a divorce from his wife Flavia Augustus. The document is not signed by either party or by any legal official. When we examined the document from Ada's box, however, we discovered a signed and witnessed document in which Maximus transferred ownership of his estate to Flavia, this is unusual, but not unheard of at that time. "

"Sorry, why would Maximus do that if Flavia would not divorce him? I don't understand." Said a frowning Harriet.

"We may never know exactly, but perhaps he intended to return to Britannia and never return, anyway, there is a handwritten addendum, to the signed document, added sometime later and signed by Flavia Augustus."

"What did it say?" asked Harriet, moving to the edge of her seat.

"My dear Odell, it is my profound wish Tamm should have this, and all it entails, my situation is tenuous, to say the least, it is unlikely I will ever take ownership, but it is my sincere wish following Maximus's untimely death, Tamm will one day claim his inheritance should he wish to do so." Always at your service Flavia Augustus."

"Wow, so Odell was Tamm's mother and Maximus, his father. The tone of the letter suggests Flavia and Odell knew each other too, it's fascinating, is there any further information about Marcus?" Asked Harriet.

"We don't currently know any more about Marcus, but Cyrus has kindly agreed to keep looking, "replied Ada.

It was at that moment Harriet noticed Cyrus and Ada exchange looks.

"Harriet dear, there's something Cyrus and I wish to raise with you," said Ada holding Harriet's gaze.

"Oh, yes? Are you two about to gang up on me?" Laughed Harriet.

"Absolutely not, but we know a little of the inner turmoil you've been experiencing of late with the disappearance of Henry. As you know he is one of my best friends and I feel his loss intensely, but not like you do," said Cyrus.

"So, we would like you to consider travelling to Yemen, in search of him," said Ada taking a large bite of cake.

"Bless you both, I have hidden my turmoil badly, and, as much as I would like to and please believe I want to go with every fibre of my body, I have responsibilities at home and at work, which makes such a trip impossible."

"Where there's a will, there's a way," said Ada.

"Indeed, sometimes, Harriet, you must take a leap of faith, it is all arranged, Mike is to accompany you; Derek Wynn has authorised unpaid leave for you both. I will finance your trip, no arguing, and your mother Jane and Nick's parents will be on hand should Amelia need them, but Kate Squires will come and stay at yours, so I think their services are unlikely to be required. Both Ben and Amelia have been consulted and fully support you going. So, you see, it's all been taken care of." Harriet looked at the floor, trying her hardest to compose herself.

"I don't know how to thank you, I didn't dare believe I might be able to go, I am indebted."

"There's just one thing I feel I must say before you go, Yemen is a country in the grip of civil war, it is a confusing, noisy, and dangerous place. You will fly from Heathrow to Sanaa, the international airport in Yemen, on Thursday. A man called Abdulaziz will meet you at the airport, he's a friend of mine, he will be your driver and guide. The following day you will meet with a representative from Médecins Sans Frontières, after which you will set off on your search, some of your journey will be by vehicle, some on foot. It is 125 miles to Taiz from Sanaa. I have briefed Mike; he has all the documentation required, oh yes, and one last thing, dress moderately and make sure you cover your head with a scarf, you need to blend in and not stand out, please take excellent care of yourself." Cyrus walked across and hugged Harriet long and hard.

"You are an extraordinary detective and woman, Harriet, and I have grown to care deeply for you over the last few months, I look forward immensely to hearing about your adventures on your return and, of course, to meeting your Henry. "The two women hugged before Harriet took her leave.

Yemen was every bit as chaotic and confusing as Cyrus had warned, Harriet and Mike stuck close to their guide, grateful that Abdulaziz spoke fluent English. He was a painfully thin man, Harriet estimated in his early forties, clean shaven, with beady black eyes, thinning short afro hair and a thin black moustache covering his top lip.

At their first meeting, he explained a little of what was going on in his country.

"I give you a bit of a history lesson. The Houthi threw out the Yemeni government in 2014 and sank us into a civil war, it has been raging since, the Houthi are a militant group, they have spread their power across many of the cities in the north. With support from Iran, they have blockaded Taiz, many of the roads in Taiz and Yemen generally are closed. Journey's that used to take fifteen minutes can now take many hours. Harriet, as a woman you may find at checkpoints you are asked to name a male guardian, that will be me, they will not let you continue otherwise."

It was the day after their meeting with MSF and they now knew the route Henry and his team had planned to take to Taiz. Abdulaziz had insisted on an early start and, having secured an old four by four vehicle, instructed Harriet and Mike to stay by it while he dashed to the local market, such as it was, for supplies.

Mike leant against the vehicle smoking a local cigarette.

"I swear this thing is made from animal dung," he said pulling a face, Harriet laughed.

The street they were waiting in was busy, dusty, and noisy. Harriet tried to take in her surroundings and make sense of them. Old stone buildings with white, yellow, and pink plaster, framed a small square, where a group of old men were chewing quat and debating. A myriad of vehicles queued next to them on the grimy road crawling their way out of the city. Skinny dogs ran in and out of the queuing vehicles, there was the odd sound of normal daily life, a crying baby, a stall holder calling out to potential customers, the hint of meat cooking. Harriet looked for, but could not see, other women on the street; the gender inequality was obvious for all to see.

It all happened quickly, gun shots and the revving of engines nearby, Mike grabbed Harriet's arm and pulled her down to the ground behind the nearside of their vehicle. It was impossible to see what was going on.

"Bloody Hell! Do we stay here and wait for Abdulaziz? Or do we try to make our way back to MSF Headquarters?" He asked.

"Can you reach our bags from the vehicle do you think?"

"I'll try, hold the door open for me, and I'll crawl onto the backseat."

Mike slowly crawled into the car, as more gun shots rang out, accompanied by nearby shouting. Using the tips of his fingers, he managed to retrieve their document bag, but then the offside of their vehicle was sprayed with bullets.

"Keep low Mike and run," whispered Harriet, shaking violently.

They ran from the vehicle to a side road adjacent to the main thoroughfare, hearts beating through their chests, they took shelter in the doorway of a derelict building.

"Mike, you are not going to believe this, but I think, no I'm sure I've just seen Nick." Harriet felt faint.

"Nick who?" asked a wide-eyed Mike.

"My Nick, my estranged husband, your ex-boss," snapped Harriet.

"Where? Really?"

"Yes, over there," Harriet pointed to a sandy pink building on the corner of the next street."

"Impossible, he's in the Mediterranean somewhere, it's the stress."

"Perhaps."

A battered yellow jeep pulled up alongside, the driver wound down the window, Harriet's mouth fell open, a small gasp escaped before she covered her mouth with both hands.

"Quick! Jump in, jump in now!" shouted the driver.

With less than a split second to decide, Harriet grabbed the door handle and wrenched the back door open, "Mike, get in now!" Mike obliged; as Harriet flung herself after him, the vehicle sped up ramming its way past several slow-moving cars, bullets hailing down on it.

Acknowledgements:

Thank you to my husband for your continuing support and encouragement.

Printed in Great Britain
by Amazon